WISHFUL THINKING

THE WISHING TREE SERIES, BOOK 9

KAY BRATT

CONTENTS

Praise for Kay Bratt — v
Also By Kay Bratt — xv

Chapter 1 — 1
Chapter 2 — 16
Chapter 3 — 26
Chapter 4 — 31
Chapter 5 — 45
Chapter 6 — 59
Chapter 7 — 70
Chapter 8 — 78
Chapter 9 — 87
Chapter 10 — 101
Chapter 11 — 113
Chapter 12 — 120
Chapter 13 — 127
Chapter 14 — 136

From the Author — 155
About the Author — 159

PRAISE FOR KAY BRATT

"Quinn Maguire has grown up believing that she knows the truth about her complicated childhood. But when her mother dies shortly after revealing an earth-shaking family secret, everything changes in an instant. Kay Bratt beautifully draws the story of a daughter returning to Maui—the enchanted land that she believes holds the key to her past—where she unlocks a promising future she never could have imagined. Full of secrets, love and gorgeous settings, *True to Me* is the ultimate escape." —**Kristy Woodson Harvey, bestselling author of *Slightly South of Simple***

"Heartfelt and brimming with lively characters, *True to Me* is a poignant reminder of the meaning of family, the importance of truth, and the power of forgiveness. Perfect for fans of Christine Nolfi and Cathy Lamb." — **Sonja Yoerg, *Washington Post* bestselling author of *True Places***

"Bratt writes a beautiful tale of family which grabbed me from the very first page. Quinn, mourning the loss of her mother, must travel to Maui in search of her roots. Leaving behind her fiancé Ethan, she is drawn to the island's rich history and the locals who welcome her into their world. Woven between the pages is the deep mystery of Quinn's past, and the DNA test that leads her to a family she never knew. Bratt takes the reader on a heartfelt journey of family and forgiveness while Quinn teaches us about those we should let in and those we should let go. For at the very core of the novel is the rare gift of being true to one's self." — **Rochelle B. Weinstein, *USA Today* bestselling author**

"*Wish Me Home* has all the trademarks of a Kay Bratt novel: a heartwarming story that nourishes the soul, beloved characters, and a plot that kept me turning pages. Without shying away from the harshness of life, Bratt has managed to create a world in which kindness and goodness prevail. My advice to those who haven't read this book yet? Find your comfy reading spot, get your beverage of choice, and sink into the world of *Wish Me Home*. You'll be glad you did." —**Karen McQuestion, bestselling author of *Hello Love***

"In this inspiring story of a woman's search for the deepest wish of her heart, Bratt paints a realistic portrait of the dark side of the foster care system, while simultaneously reminding us that there is always hope, and that home and family can be found in unexpected places." —**Kerry Anne King, bestselling author of** *Closer Home* **and** *I Wish You Happy*

"With its resilient protagonist, secret that kept me guessing, dog I wish I could adopt in real life, and story that tugged at my heart, Kay Bratt's *Wish Me Home* grabbed me and held me all the way to its heartfelt resolution. Readers who enjoy novels like Vanessa Diffenbaugh's *The Language of Flowers* will find it a delight!" —**Nancy Star, bestselling author of** *Sisters One, Two, Three*

"A baring-of-the-soul emotional story that leaves you with a heart full of love and hope." —**Carolyn Brown,** *New York Times* **bestselling author, for** *Dancing with the Sun*

"*In Dancing With the Sun*, a mother and daughter are forced to lean on each other for survival in the wilderness while learning to let go of years of grief and guilt. Readers will relate to Kay Bratt's depiction of a mother's love and her courage in protecting her daughter. Ultimately, though, this novel is a page-turner that will pull on your heartstrings and affirm your faith in humanity." —**Karen McQuestion, bestselling author of** *Hello Love*

"*Dancing with the Sun* is an evocative story of emotional

and physical survival in the harshest of terrains. Mother and wife Sadie Harlan is struggling silently with grief when she and her daughter go missing in Yosemite. Away from the world and focused on keeping her daughter alive, Sadie embarks on an unforgettable journey through loss and guilt to find forgiveness, healing, and strength. Book clubs will love the powerful message of this unique novel." —**Barbara Claypole White, bestselling author of *The Perfect Son* and *The Promise Between Us***

"*Dancing with the Sun* is an endearing, emotional tale filled with the perfect mix of poignant family heartaches, unshakable mother-daughter love, and a dose of adventure in a dramatic, vivid setting that will sweep you away until the very last page. Don't miss it." —**Julianne MacLean, *USA Today* bestselling author**

"Whether facing the natural terrors of Yosemite or the internal pains of an unforgiven past, this mother-daughter story is beautifully written and relatable as one woman faces a mother's greatest fear—losing yet another child. Kay Bratt delivers on all levels in this emotional and tense story of loss and resilience." —**Emily Bleeker, Amazon Charts and *Wall Street Journal* bestselling author**

"Nothing like a harrowing, life-threatening, and completely unplanned hike through Yosemite's backcountry to make you face years of grief and guilt head on. Kay Bratt pulls this off masterfully in *Dancing with the Sun*, an emotional mother-daughter tale of love, forgiveness, and renewal. Book clubs will love Bratt's latest!" —**Kerry Lonsdale, Amazon Charts and *Wall Street Journal* bestselling author**

"In *Dancing With The Sun*, Kay Bratt captures a mother-daughter relationship with an authenticity rarely seen in novels. Highly emotional, heartfelt, and bristling with tension on every page, this is a story not easily forgotten." —**Bette Lee Crosby, *USA Today* bestselling author**

"*The Scavenger's Daughters* is the kind of novel I'd love to write, but never could. Simply told but beautifully rendered, the reader is swiftly transported into the hearts and lives of a Chinese family after the Cultural Revolution. Powerful and poignant, this story captures the heart of humanity. This is the kind of book that will get shared by friends and chosen by book clubs. A phenomenal story of life and love." —**Karen McQuestion, bestselling author of *The Long Way Home***

"*No Place Too Far* is Kay Bratt at her best. Free up some time, find somewhere quiet, and dive into this story of Maggie, Quinn, the challenges they face, and the people who love them. Once again, Bratt tackles complex contemporary issues with remarkable agility and compassion, and it's an absolute pleasure to be along for this ride. And because Bratt is a master of location, it's even more of a pleasure when the ride takes place on Maui. For a few brief moments, I forgot all about errands and laundry and the minivan and soaked up Hawaii, in all its glorious heritage and beauty." —**Lea Geller, author of** *Trophy Life*

"*No Place Too Far* is the perfect blend of suspense mixed with a magical setting and characters we care deeply about. I loved Maggie and Quinn and rooted for them until the final page. Kay Bratt is a masterful storyteller, and the story's pacing and descriptions of Maui left me always wanting more. Highly recommended for book clubs!" —**Anita Abriel, international bestselling author of** *The Light After the War*

"For two women who live in paradise, their lives are anything but idyllic. Best friends Quinn and Maggie have spent the past year trying to outrun dangers from their pasts—one a stalker, the other family secrets. But now both pasts have caught up to them, and the two friends will have to decide if they should keep running or stand up and fight. In this page-turning drama, Bratt has created two strong, dynamic female characters who readers will be sure to root for." —**Amanda Prowse, bestselling author of** *The Girl in the Corner*

"In this delicious drama set against the backdrop of paradise, Kay Bratt weaves a suspenseful story about finding the courage to fight for happiness, forgiveness, and love. I delighted in the enchanting descriptions of Maui, and I rooted for the characters as if they were friends." —**Cynthia Ellingsen, bestselling author of *The Lighthouse Keeper*, for *No Place Too Far***

Wishful Thinking… Copyright © 2022 by Kay Bratt

All rights reserved. No part of this book may be reproduced or transmitted in any form or by any means, electronic or mechanical including photocopying, recording, or by any information storage and retrieval system without the written permission of the author, except for the use of brief quotations in a book review.

For permissions contact the author directly via electronic mail: kay@Kaybratt.com

https://kaybratt.com
Facebook: https://www.facebook.com/KayBratt
Twitter: @Kay_Bratt
Instagram: @Kay_Bratt

Wishful Thinking… is a work of fiction. Names, characters, places and incidents either are products of the author's imagination or are used fictitiously. Any resemblance to actual events, locales, entities, or persons, living or dead, is entirely coincidental.

Published in the United States by Red Thread Publishing
ISBN xxx-x-xxxxxx-xx-x (paperback) ISBN
FIRST EDITION
Cover by Elizabeth Mackey Graphic Design

For our wonderful readers in My Book Friends

ALSO BY KAY BRATT

WISH ME HOME

True To Me

No Place too Far

Into the Blue

All (my) Dogs Go to Heaven

Silent Tears; A Journey of Hope in a Chinese Orphanage

Chasing China; A Daughter's Quest for Truth

Mei Li and the Wise Laoshi

Eyes Like Mine

The Bridge

A Thread Unbroken

Train to Nowhere

The Palest Ink

The Scavenger's Daughters

Tangled Vines

Bitter Winds

Red Skies

CHAPTER 1

Coco Baines couldn't feel any more out of place than she did when she had to step aside to allow two women pass her in the locker room of the Linden Falls Fitness gym. They didn't even pause in their chattering. To them she was invisible—merely a faceless blob that magically moved aside for them to pass in all their svelte, snazzy-workout-clothed gorgeousness. Coco obviously wasn't worthy of a greeting, a polite 'excuse me' or even an acknowledgement that she was a living, breathing human. Why? Because she wasn't svelte, and she sure didn't dress snazzy.

The two looked to be wearing matching outfits from the famous Kate Hudson's workout line or something like it, while Coco was trying to blend in with her faded baggy sweatpants and oversized t-shirt. Clothes that would help camouflage the twenty-five brutal pounds that weren't welcome on her hips. And the extra five in her breasts.

That's why you're here, hiding in a small town where no one knows you while you transform yourself. Suck it up, Buttercup.

She coached herself out of the self-annihilating mood that was descending upon her and left the locker room and the gossip-fest behind. She didn't care what they prattled on about. All she heard was that someone named Susan Wilbanks got a new and huge diamond for their anniversary and how obscene she thought it was to be showing it around the charity luncheon when they were discussing helping the homeless.

And that's why you don't have girlfriends.

Because Coco would bet dollars to donuts that the girl who was putting 'ole Susan down was probably one of her best friends. Back-stabbing at its best.

Best friends were over-rated.

Coco quietly made her way to the closest rack of barbells. An elderly woman sat on the bench in front of them, sipping a glass of red wine. Diamond earrings hung from her ears and her pantsuit looked expertly ironed all the way down to the ankles, that were crossed and wearing very fancy ballet flats.

She waved her hand at Coco. "Don't mind me. I'm only here because my doctor said I need to do physical therapy to get my hip back up to par. I promised him I'd go to the gym at least twice a week for a month or so. But I didn't promise him I'd do anything, except watch the young 'uns pump iron. But he's right, I feel better already!" She grinned and held her glass up in a salute. "I'm Agnes, by the way."

Coco laughed at her spunk. "Hi, Agnes. I'm Coco. Enjoy your workout!"

She moved around the tiny woman to get to the barbells. Someone had loaded one with small weights and she took it and began doing arm lifts while she watched Tweedle Dee and Tweedle Dum emerge from the locker room and begin posing in front of the mirrors as they snapped selfies.

Coco wished she could snap *them*.

It wasn't completely true that she didn't have friends. She just didn't have friends that she saw or spoke with very often anymore. She worked too much.

After spending five years as an editorial assistant, doing research, writing reports and basically being a servant to the editorial staff members at the station and doing most of their grunt work for them, she'd finally been promoted to field reporter. For the next five years until now, she'd burned the candle at both ends, researching and writing articles and interviewing people from every sort of background you can imagine.

Then a position came open as a news anchor. The very job she'd worked so hard to get and wanted so badly. She applied and had all but celebrated the promotion because she just had to get it—she was the only one at the station who was qualified and not only that, but she'd done her time in the trenches. It was her turn.

Her moment.

She felt her pulse quicken and began pumping the small weights harder. Faster.

It was a moment, all right. A moment of complete humiliation when the station manager Frank sat her down and in what she thought was going to be a congratulatory meeting of telling her she had the job, instead he told her she wasn't the image the station wanted to present to the public.

Because her record and background were spotless, and if she said so herself, her eyes and her smile were nice enough, it was only after an awkward silence that fell upon them did she get what he was saying.

"You mean I'm too fat for the viewers?"

Of course, he started backtracking quickly. He didn't want a lawsuit.

"Now I didn't say that, but since you brought it up, don't you think you'd feel better if you were more.. well… fit? And you'd be able to shop that bargain dress shop downtown for the perfect outfits to wear on air. I mean—for when and if you get the position. Though I just want you to know that I've got a few more applicants to talk to before I decide. We still have three months before Dixie goes out on extended maternity leave and the position opens up."

A few more applicants, her butt.

Frank didn't have anyone else on the payroll who wanted the job. He'd have to pay a head-hunter to get someone there that was anywhere near as qualified as

Coco—though she was sure that someone wouldn't weigh any more than a hundred pounds soaking wet.

He had no plans of giving her the job. As a matter of fact, it was his suggestion that she take some time away from work, to finally use up more than six years of vacation time she'd never taken. He wanted her out of the way. Probably couldn't look at her, knowing what a jerk he was and how he'd done her wrong.

"Yeah, I'll take my time off. But I'm coming back," she told him.

As a last dig, on her first day away he had emailed her to say that he didn't take the staffing decisions lightly, and how it was his responsibility to put someone in place as a local public personality that would be a role model to the community—someone who could present and promote a healthy lifestyle.

Coco was so angry. Not only had she done everything he'd asked her to, but she'd also gained her master's degree in Broadcast Journalism just so that she'd have the upper hand on most applicants who only had a Bachelors. Frank had encouraged her to do it, then declined her request for employer tuition support. Coco had lived on practically nothing but noodles for two years to pay her own way. It was more than financially hard, too. Between working fifty hours a week at the station and getting through her classes, she'd surrendered every tiny bit of personal life she had left.

It had been worth it, she thought, because she got that diploma.

However, in that endeavor she'd also sacrificed her

only long-term relationship. She had met Travis when he'd subbed from another station. He was one of the best cameramen in the industry and they'd hit it off right away. He was probably the best looking and the most successful guy she'd ever known, and everyone had said they looked like a power couple. On his arm she'd felt gorgeous, and it was embarrassing, but she'd flooded social media with photos of them together. He was the tall, dark and handsome guy with a physique that he spent a lot of time perfecting. Not surprisingly, he'd been a football star in high school and college, just missing a chance to play professional. But he'd used his charm to pivot and make a name for himself in the media circles as a sought-after cameraman.

She really thought she'd marry him eventually, but two years in, he told her she was too ambitious for the sort of wife he wanted. Ironic considering her ambition is what he'd said had attracted him to her in the first place.

Suddenly he couldn't understand that ambition equaled success and success could be the foundation of their life together.

They just weren't on the same page; he'd said as he packed his things and then disappeared from her life forever. Not two weeks later she'd seen him posing for a couple photos on Instagram with a sexy little administrative assistant at his station that he always claimed he couldn't stand. She'd instantly deleted her social media accounts. It was easier than having to go through and look for each photo with him to take them down one-by-one.

Then Coco had done what she does best and pulled her bootstraps up and focused on her career even more. That was about the time she'd changed her name at Frank's insistence because he said that *Courtney* was over-used in television, especially seeing how it belonged to a Kardashian. Coco hadn't corrected him that the celebrity in question was Courtney with a K. She simply conceded and took the name he suggested.

Coco.

To her it sounded like a stripper hanging on a pole.

Or something topped with marshmallows that Grandma served Christmas carolers at her door.

And now Coco was angry *and* hungry.

Before she could really lose it, someone approached her. Coco took the much-needed break and lowered the barbells.

"Hi, I'm Pam, a trainer here. I don't think we've met?" the pretty brunette asked politely. Coco saw her toned arms and legs and felt a surge of envy.

She tried to hide her struggle to catch her breath. "I'm Coco. I'm new to Linden Falls."

"Just moved in?" Pam asked, handing her one of the bottles of water she held.

"Thank you," Coco said. "No—not going to live here. I'm on a hiatus from work. I took a few months off to.. um… well, just to take some time off."

She opened the bottle and took a long swig.

Pam smiled. "That sounds nice. Where are you staying?"

Coco sighed. The people of Linden Falls were nosy.

"I took a room at the inn."

Now the smile got huge. "Oh, you'll love it over there. Neva, Janie, and the girls will take superb care of you. Have you had one of their meals yet? You'll just die over the cooking and baking that goes on under that roof. Both Neva and Carly are amazing cooks."

"No, I haven't." Coco tried to keep the frustration out of her tone. Pam was nice. She just didn't know. "I have some dietary restrictions, so I'll be preparing my own food. Ms. Cabot was nice enough to say I could use the kitchen when they aren't in it."

Pam nodded. "Oh. Okay. Well, can I give you some pointers about your workout?"

"Sorry, I can't afford a trainer," Coco said.

"Oh no. I wasn't offering my paid services. This is on the house. I just don't want to see you hurt yourself. If you're going to use that much aggression when you work out, let's try the dumbbell punch. You've got the right size dumbbells so now let's get you formed out."

Coco felt her face flame red. Everyone in the building probably knew she didn't belong and darn sure didn't know what she was doing.

Pam picked up a few of the other small dumbbells and took a stance beside Coco.

"See, do it like this. You want to do one arm at a time. Stand up straight and hold them both at your waist, and then slowly and with full control, punch forward at face height."

She did a few very graceful punches then turned to Coco.

"Your turn."

Coco imitated her and had to admit, even though she probably looked like a blind polar bear in a fist fight, it felt better than the random up and down frantic way she'd been doing it before. Also, a lot less dangerous.

"Do ten reps and then return to your starting position and do the other arm."

"Thanks," Coco said. "I appreciate the tip."

"Of course. And if you tell me what your workout goals are, I can probably show you a few more easy things to do."

Coco stopped her punches and turned to Pam.

"I need to lose weight in my hips and my—well.. my.." she glanced down at her shirt.

"Breasts?" Pam said, matching Coco's whisper.

"Yes. And I need to do it in twelve weeks or less."

"Hmm.. well, that's doable, depending on how much weight you want to lose. Do you have a number?"

"Thirty," Coco whispered, feeling her face flame again.

Pam stood back and looked her up and down. "Thirty? Are you sure? That's a lot off your frame and it's going to take some work if you really want to get it done in under three months. You'll have to exercise hard, change your eating habits, and really put the work in."

"I'll do anything. I mean it. Anything."

She tried not to notice the sad look that took over Pam's face before she covered it up with a smile.

"Well, okay then. Look, this is what I'll do. If you're coming back tomorrow, you and I can sit down and talk, then I'll have you a fitness plan worked up on paper by the end of the week. We need to combine a healthy diet with cardio and strength training, but in a safe way."

"Really? You'll do a plan for free? Wow," Coco said.

"Yes. I do that sometimes for people I feel passionate about. It also helps me stretch my trainer skills. Good homework for me."

"I don't even know what to say. I mean, thank you. So much."

Pam nodded. "You're welcome. Now for today, cardio is your best bet to burn calories. Have you ever been on a treadmill?"

"Yes, I have. It's been a long time, though."

"It's like riding a bicycle. Come on."

Coco followed, feeling completely exposed as Pam led her through the gym and to the wall of mirrors with treadmills lined up in front.

Pam beckoned at a treadmill at the end, right next to a gorgeous honey-blonde Stepford wife that was prettily jogging while using her pointy finger to scroll up on her phone. She had earbuds in her ears and a bracelet of pearls on her wrist. Big, fat, expensive ones.

Who wore pearls to the gym?

"That's Daisy Crawford," Pam leaned in and whispered. "She thinks she's royalty. Just ignore her. In five minutes, she'll be out of your way and batting her eyelashes at her trainer while he spots her over at the leg lift machine. She never deviates from her routine."

Coco got up on the treadmill and Daisy shot her a disgusted look as though her zen moment was being disturbed.

Pam got between them, blocking Daisy's hateful glare.

"Okay, here's the start button. Since it's been a while, I suggest a three-minute set starting at just 3 mph. You'll walk for one minute, then jog for a minute, and then run a minute. I'll leave you alone but after that, if you feel good about it, you can do it again but increase your speed by a few mph."

"Sounds easy enough," Coco said.

"It is, and don't worry if you don't want to increase the speed. Tomorrow you may feel different and will do them faster. Or not. It's okay to just listen to your body."

I don't have time to listen to my body.

Pam nodded and walked away. She was so nice. Thank goodness the gym wasn't only prima donnas and muscle heads. She hit the start button and began walking. That was easy enough and she gently turned her walk into a jog at the second minute mark. She peeked at Daisy Crawford from her peripheral view and hoped that she couldn't see how much Coco was starting to sweat. At the three-minute mark she began a run. It would only be sixty seconds.

She could do anything for sixty seconds.

When the clock got down to just twenty seconds left, Coco felt like she was going to have a heart attack. The sweat dripped off her forehead and rolled down her nose, and the crack of her butt felt wet and itchy.

Ten seconds.

Suddenly Daisy Crawford pulled the ear bud from her ear and leaned over.

"That's way too slow to burn any calories."

She hit a few buttons and though Coco wanted to throat punch Daisy at the sudden surge in speed, she wouldn't give her the satisfaction of stopping.

Run, Coco, run.

Five seconds left.

Her boobs threatened to give her a black eye and her cleavage felt like a swamp, but she kept running.

She would've been able to do it, too. If that Dingbat Daisy hadn't reached over yet again and hit another button, sending the treadmill into God-only-knows what speed and sending Coco clutching the handrails to keep from flying off the back.

"Oh no," Daisy said, coming to a stop.

But instead of helping her out by stopping Coco's machine, Daisy held her hand to her mouth and watched as Coco was taken down to a squat, then was dragged along the treadmill for at least five seconds before Pam's sprint across the room brought her there like Wonder woman. She pulled the emergency switch, sending Coco catapulting backward onto the floor, her legs in the air like she was in the middle of the most embarrassing gynecological visit on the planet.

"Are you okay?" Pam exclaimed. She knelt beside Coco; her expression genuinely concerned.

No, she wasn't okay. There was burning going on somewhere, though everything was hurting too much to pinpoint from where exactly. She wished that the gym floor would open and swallow her whole, but of course she wasn't that lucky.

She put her legs down, sat up and glared at Daisy, who did an impressive imitation of an apologetic person.

"I thought you wanted to go faster," she said through the fingers of her hand that still covered her mouth. Her accent was a sickeningly sweet southern drawl. *Or pretend drawl.*

"You never touch anyone else's equipment in this gym," Pam scolded her, then held a hand down to Coco.

"I'm fine. I can get up," Coco said, though she felt a bit dizzy.

"Wait a second," Pam said, then jerked on Coco's pant leg, pulling it from the machine. "You were caught."

When Coco stood, she noticed that the gym had gone completely silent. Everyone had stopped their workout and was staring at her.

A very handsome guy at the row of stationary bikes was collecting flies with his open mouth as he gawked.

Even Tweedle Dee and Dum had stopped their prancing around and stood there watching, smirks spread across their faces.

Coco noticed that one of them had her phone aimed straight at her. "I can't wait for this to go viral," the tallest one said.

Before Coco could even react to that bit of news, Daisy made a guttural sound.

"Oh my Gawd," she exclaimed. "You can see your granny panties. And they're lime green!"

"Stop it right now," Pam said to the bimbo taking the video, and repeated it at Daisy. "You all need to grow up."

As if the scene wasn't horrific enough, Coco looked down to see that her jogging pants were ripped down the side, giving everyone quite a show. Now she wished she wouldn't have kept putting off buying new underwear.

She felt something wet going down her leg.

"*And* she's peed herself," Daisy declared, as if announcing the final to a horse race.

Agnes jumped up and grabbed a towel from the bench where she sat, then surprisingly fast for someone with a hip problem, she scampered over and wrapped it around Coco.

"Don't pay them any mind," she said, waving at everyone to stop staring. "I do it all the time."

Coco was no longer thinking about the gym rats. Now she was wondering how fast the video of her falling, displaying her less-than-attractive underthings, and then Daisy pointing out that in the chaos, she'd lost her bladder was going to land in the hands of Frank, the boss who loved a funny viral video—the boss who would have yet one more reason not to give her Karen's job.

Just when she thought life couldn't get any worse.

"I am so, so sorry," Pam murmured. "But please, Coco, don't feel bad. There are a lot of accidents here. Sweaty people and electrical equipment always bring about some of the most embarrassing moments. It happens to all of us."

Coco hadn't yet found her tongue. She wasn't even able to move.

She wasn't embarrassed.

Nope—that wasn't the word.

She was mortified.

Down to her very core.

And she would never…

Ever..

Ever, return to the gym again.

CHAPTER 2

*J*anie pulled the tray of gemstones out from the display case and set them on top for Coco—their latest extended stay guest—to look at. The energy coming off her needed work. A lot of it, too. She didn't know if she even had a stone in stock that could penetrate the vibes the woman was putting out. But she'd opened the shop to help people in crisis, and that was what she intended to do. Or at least try to do.

"If you can tell me a bit about what you are wanting to make better in your life, I can point you to the right stone," Janie said.

"Why can't I just pick? Your sign outside says *YOUR INTUITION LED YOU HERE*. Shouldn't I let my intuition pick the stone?"

Janie smiled gently. She'd met Coco that morning in the kitchen, where they'd discussed protein shakes. Coco had declined any offers of food, saying that she was only going to eat one meal a day. Janie wasn't a fitness expert, but she did know that eating only one meal a day could mess with a person's body clock and affect their sleeping cycles as well as their metabolism, and not in a good way.

But she wasn't about to give unsolicited health advice.

"Yes, that's the name of the shop and intuition is definitely one way to do it. But each stone represents different things. For instance, this one," Janie picked up a light green stone. "It's Amazonite and it's good to clear out traumas you might have locked in your body that are deterring your harmonious balance. It's for courage."

"I have plenty of courage," she said.

Janie picked up a purple stone. "And the amethyst here is a protection against fear and feelings of guilt. It will help alleviate any connected anxiety."

Coco looked impatient. "I can assure you, I've done nothing to feel guilty about. Though I know a few people who should be carrying that stone."

Janie put it back. "Okay, I think I've made my point clear. They all serve different issues. But if you just want one because it's pretty, that's fine too."

The woman paused. "Well, if I tell you some details and you help me pick one, will it work faster?"

"I can't guarantee the speed or the outcome of using crystals to help cleanse certain parts of your life. Once they leave the store, it's all about how you use them," Janie said. "I can tell you this, though. Whichever one you choose you'll need to look after it with all the love and intention you can muster up."

"I really have no idea how to do what you just said. I'm not really a believer in this sort of stuff."

Then why are you even in my shop?

Janie took a deep breath and reminded herself that everyone has struggles that no one knows about. But she couldn't work miracles. "Then maybe this isn't the right time for you to try this. Your crystal should be like your talisman against whatever the world has to throw at you. But if you don't believe in its power, then it won't work at all."

"Is this some sort of witchcraft?" Coco asked, looking worried.

Janie picked up the tray and put it back into the display case. Enough was enough. She'd been through enough soul-searching and anxiety over being her true self than to have to put up with it anymore. From now on, if someone wanted to think she was some kind of woo-woo freak, they could do it from afar.

"No, actually it isn't. But you're free to believe what you want. People have turned to crystals for healing since mankind was put on this planet. Gems and stones are treasures of Mother Earth and they're infused with elemental energy from the sun and the moon. Even from the oceans and mountains. Used in the right way they can transfer all that healing power back to us."

"I'm sorry. I don't mean to be insulting, I promise! I have just never heard about them."

Janie shrugged. "I can't tell you why you've never

heard of them. They were used by warriors and priests in their attire, and many ancient tribes centered their daily lives around them. Healing crystals have a very long history."

"I just hope it works. I'm desperate."

"So—do you have one in mind? I can tell you about more of the others if you'd like?" Janie pulled the tray back out again and set it down. She'd give her one more chance. But if she started throwing around the witch-word again, it was over.

Coco leaned in and looked around before she whispered. "I need something for weight loss. Something that works fast."

Janie plucked a blue-green stone from the case and held it out to Coco. "Well, I don't think a stone is going to work that way but look at this one. It's a Blue Apatite and it's said to work wonders for metabolism and for coaxing your mental state to crave healthy foods. Some say it helps with hunger pangs, too."

"I'll take it. Just tell me how to use it, please."

Janie quickly walked her to the register and rang up the purchase.

Coco stopped to look at the dandelion display. Janie was quite proud of how colorful and inviting it was, and that it was the work of a family project. Even Neva had helped Janie and the girls to go around and snip off dandelion heads. Then one batch at a time they'd made it into body balm, soap, and even a very good facial serum. Together they'd come up with a design for the sticker label, and the vintage look of it felt just right.

Obviously not to Coco, who moved on and pointed to something else.

"Those are tarot cards. Animal version."

"Oh. For predicting the future?"

Janie shook her head. "No. That's a common misconception. They are really to offer spiritual guidance to the person that receives the card. They help you connect to your inner wisdom, especially about a specific situation going on in your life."

Coco plucked a set from the top and set them beside the stone, then fished out her credit card and handed it over. "I'll take them."

Janie hid her surprise. "Great. Let me know if you need any help reading them. Just remember it's about exploring a question about the self, then picking a card to help you reflect on a possible answer. You can find all kinds of guides on the internet, too. And for the stone, I'll put it in a pouch, but you can have it made into a necklace if you like. It's great to wear the stone next to your skin to kick the vibration level up," Janie said, pulling her drawer of silk pouches out and choosing a deep burgundy to put the stone into, then tucking it and the deck of cards into a bag.

She handed Coco the receipt and the bag, thanked her, and watched her walk to the front of the store, waddling like she was in pain as she poked her purchase down into her purse.

Neva reached the door first from the other side and held it open. "Why hello, Ms. Baines. So nice of you to come check out Janie's new shop. I hope you are enjoying Linden Falls."

"Hello, Ms. Cabot. Please—you can call me Coco. I'll see you later," she said, then quickly walked out of sight.

Neva continued inside; her eyebrows raised to the ceiling. "Well. Someone is not having a good day, I can sense."

Janie nodded. "Yeah, not sure what's going on with her, other than she is too critical of herself. I don't think she realizes how attractive she is. She's worried about her weight."

"What? Why, that's crazy. She's just the right size. People are so hard on themselves," Neva said. "I just wish we could all see ourselves as others see us, not how the mirror lies. I'm glad now that I followed my instinct and built her a small fire in her room. She looked like she could use some comfort, didn't she?"

"Yes, she did."

"I also left a jar of coconut oil. Not sure why but I think she'll need it."

Janie smiled. Her aunt's supernatural gift never ceased to amaze her, and she could guarantee that Coco needed that oil for something. "That was nice of you, Neva, but what are you doing here? Aren't you supposed to be getting ready to go with Henry to the Aspen Care volunteer luncheon?"

Neva waved her hand in the air. "Oh, that'll just take me a few minutes. I don't like to fuss over myself too much or he'll think I'm trying too hard."

Janie smiled. Their relationship was cute.

It was the first real courtship she'd ever seen, and it was entertaining to watch. Henry was pulling out all the stops with picking her up at the door, flowers in hand and dressed to the nines. It had been going on for a few months and it appeared that they were both perfectly happy with where they were.

"I really just wanted to see what you've done in the last few days," Neva said, then inhaled deeply when she saw the table of candles that Janie had put out that morning.

"I'm getting there. Tomorrow I'm supposed to get the shipment of sage bundles. Maybe we can use them in the inn after difficult guests."

Neva laughed. "Great idea."

"What do you think of the sign outside? I finally settled on a name for the shop."

Neva clasped her hands together, "Oh, it's perfect. Everyone will want to wander in here and find out what WISHFUL THINKING is. And I'm so glad you decided to do this, Janie. I do believe it's probably the very first thing in your life you've done totally for yourself. And it shows. You look so settled and at peace."

"I am. For the most part." It was true. The shop was something that Janie had always dreamt of doing but had never had the courage to do. In some towns, shops like hers would be very frowned upon. Word was just getting out around Linden Falls about the shop, she hadn't dealt with much backlash. Other than a few comments here and there like she'd heard minutes before.

"What could we do to make it for all parts?" Neva asked in her inquisitive way.

Since Janie had told her they were closely related, their relationship had only gotten better every day. Neva was thrilled to have family around her for the first time in her adult life, and the girls thought the sun rose on their great auntie's face.

"Oh, I don't know. I thought that once I focused on the spiritual part of my life, and keeping it balanced, instead of just the materialistic stuff, everything would feel different. And it does, to a point. But I guess I need to figure out what's going to happen with Max and me. Leaving that loose thread has me feeling incomplete. We just need to settle the terms."

Neva sighed. "And you're sure you want to go through with it?"

Janie picked up her duster and went to work on the countertop. The one that didn't need dusting at all. Finally, she turned to Neva.

"I don't think I've thanked you enough for letting me turn your attic into living space for us, so we could use this carriage house for the shop. And everything you are doing with Carly—I'm still awed that she'll be going to Paris next summer to shadow a real chef. I feel like we've stepped into a dream."

Neva came closer and opened her arms wide. Janie stepped into them and let herself be enveloped in the warmth. When they let go, Neva smiled broadly.

"See? That's how you are thanking me. You brought me family, Janie. There's nothing more priceless than having all of you under the same roof with me. And you are the sound businesswoman who has made all this happen. Before you came and helped me put other avenues of income into place with the café side and the book club teas, I was barely making it month to month. Now we have money coming in without robbing Peter to pay Paul! You'd think we dug up 'ole Mary May's money tree and planted it in our own backyard."

Janie laughed. "I still don't know if I can get on board with that story, but okay. I only know that if I had a money tree blooming every day in my yard, I'd high tail it to the first island for sale I could find and park my butt under a big umbrella, a pink drink in my hands."

"Bless her heart. I'm glad Mary finally got her life together. And I don't believe you for a minute. With that generous heart of yours, you'd be doing the same sort of thing with the money that she did. But anyway, I need to run. I'll check in with Loretta before I go and ask her to remember to give the floor in the tearoom an extra sheen for this weekend's event. And I'll let Breeze know I'm leaving, and she can watch the house for an hour or so until Roland arrives and takes over."

"Sounds good, but I think she's starting to crush on that boy," Janie said. "Someone is going to have to tell her he's a lost cause to her charms."

"Aww, let her crush. It's healthy." With that, Neva swooshed out the door, taking a swirl of vitality and kindness with her. Her aunt didn't need any magick stones, amulets, or special potions. She was the real thing and all the good stuff just oozed from her and around her.

Janie hoped one day it would all trickle down to her.

CHAPTER 3

Coco took her bag and went into the inn and slowly climbed the stairs. She'd already been up there earlier to change clothes after her debacle at the gym, and once she'd shed the gym pants, she saw why her legs burned. Somehow the treadmill fiasco had made burns on both her knees—ugly spots that resembled road rash.

Now all she wanted to do was rest and try to figure out her next steps.

She opened the door and went in, closing it softly behind her. She'd chosen the Robert Frost room, though really, she hadn't had a preference. When she'd called in to ask about an extended stay, Ms. Cabot had thought it very important that she think over her room choice and decide, and since Robert Frost sounded like the most famous of all the themes offered, she chosen it.

Now she was glad she had.

It felt like she was staying in an old English mansion house with its red-hued walls, a gorgeous four-poster bed that looked inviting with its plush pillows and thick, layered burgundy coverlets. An antique Chippendale desk took up one corner, and beckoned Coco to come and write, if she could ever get her anxiety down enough to release her muse. Even the floors looked like original hardwoods, and she was pleased to see that a small fire crackled in the fireplace.

She took her small bag she'd gotten from the shop and went to the winged-back chair to take in the comfort and warmth while she looked at her new treasures. She noticed a jar on the table beside the chair and a small note taped to the top.

Coconut oil is good for a variety of things like hair conditioning, skin care and even first aid for minor burns. Love, Neva.

Coco's face felt hot. Pam from the gym must've called and told Ms. Cabot about the incident. Soon the whole town would know. Maybe she should move on to somewhere else. A new town with a different gym.

But she really did like Linden Falls so far. And she hated gyms. Like, truly and passionately hated them with all of her being.

She'd sleep on it and decide after the humiliation of the day wasn't as prominent.

First, she wanted to at least give the stone a chance to work. She dumped it into her hand and held it tightly, closing her eyes.

Help me lose this weight.

She said it over and over in her head, making it a mantra.

When she opened her eyes, she felt ridiculous.

It was a rock.

But she was about to make herself even more ridiculous because she wanted to see what the tarot cards held in store for her. She pulled out her phone and a did a quick internet search and read the instructions.

First it said to prepare the area to set the mood using lighting and scented candles or incense. She didn't have any candles or incense, but she had lavender body spray. Quickly she went to the light switch and turned off the light, then got her spray out and waved it around the fireplace area. At least the flames in the dimness of the room helped it be more séance-like. Not that she wanted to call up any dead people or even had the ability to do so, but well—

She took a deep breath.

Calm down, Coco. This isn't rocket science.

She sat down and poured the cards out of the box, letting them fall into her hands. It said to shuffle them while thinking about her question.

How do I transform myself to be the best that I can be?

The question rolled back and forth in her mind as she shuffled, then placed the deck facedown and split it into a few other smaller decks. Then she restacked them all together into one again. For good luck, she did the process all over again, then sat back in her chair. The internet said pulling a single card was better for beginners, so with a deep breath for good luck, Coco leaned over and flipped over the first card from the deck.

Three of Wands, it read across the bottom. A woodpecker took up most of the card, depicted standing on one of three sticks that were close to a cliff's edge.

If she wasn't so worried about superstition, she'd pretend that was a trial run and just put it back and pull another. But what if the universe didn't approve? She sure didn't need to anger the cosmos and add any more stress to her life.

She studied the card more. In the background was a body of water, probably an ocean judging by the ships shown on it. Further back were mountains.

What did it mean?

Did it mean she should've opted for a cruise instead of the stay in Linden Falls? Or were the cliffs an omen that she was about to make a big mistake? Was she about to screw up her life even more?

Until this point, Coco had done everything right. Never got in trouble. Never dabbled in drugs. Limited herself to one glass of wine a night. *Okay—sometimes two.* She paid her taxes, opened doors for old ladies, and even returned shopping carts all the way to the inside of the stores when she shopped.

Oh, and she called her mother every Sunday, even when she had to force herself to pick up the phone because she knew her first question would be about Coco's love life.

Most importantly, Coco worked hard. So damn hard.

For barely any acknowledgement.

The times that she had done all the groundwork for big stories, only to hand them off to another news anchor to cover on air—it was defeating. When was it going to be her turn?

Suddenly she felt tears threaten to spring to her eyes. She blinked them away, angry at herself for being weak. Crying was for babies—not for the power businesswoman she aimed to be.

And looking at a piece of cardboard for clues about her life was silly.

She jumped up from the chair, determined not to let herself sulk. If she wasn't going to return to the gym, she needed to burn calories in another way. First up was a brisk walk around the town square while she brainstormed what to do next.

But first—the coconut oil.

Those treadmill burns weren't going to heal themselves.

CHAPTER 4

Janie listened to Carly talk and watched her put the last touches of creamy caramel frosting on the platter of zucchini cupcakes. The Winey Widows book club ladies were going to be thrilled at their scrumptious treats as they discussed their weekly read. The ladies had decided to have some of their meetings in the inn's tearoom after testing some of their new concoctions. They weren't giving up meeting at the Town Square bookstore altogether, only just booking the tearoom a few times a year going forward.

Agnes told Janie that a new setting also gave them a reason to dress up a bit more, just in case they saw any eligible bachelors visiting from out of town. She'd winked dramatically as though she was kidding, but Janie wasn't so sure.

The ladies had a much more active social life than she did. Hers was non-existent these days. And when the divorce was final, she still didn't see it getting any better. She had no interest in anything more than the girls, the inn, and now her new shop.

"I'll have to have a signature dish and I can't decide what to go for," Carly said.

"Oh—I'm sorry. What are you talking about?"

"Mom…you aren't listening! This is important."

"Okay, you said signature. You need me to sign something?" Janie faltered. The girls hated it when she got lost in her own thoughts.

"A signature *dish*. I need to be thinking of a signature dish, Mom." Carly sighed dramatically and took the frosting bowl to the sink. She turned the water on and watched the bowl fill up.

"Sure you do, honey. But not yet. Isn't that after a few years of culinary school? First you have to finish your last year in high school before we jump to the next crisis."

She got an eye roll as a response.

Carly was her serious one. Always intent on staying focused, working toward goals and doing big things. Anxious when she couldn't line things up exactly how she wanted to. On the other hand, her youngest daughter Breeze, was just like her name said, she moved along like a gentle breeze and didn't let anything get her flustered.

At this moment Breeze was sitting outside on the back steps, quietly watching the progress of a line of ants working together to carry a dead dragonfly to their abode.

"Yes, but Verity told me it'll take years to perfect a signature dish," Carly said.

Neva chose that moment to saunter in, still rosy in the cheeks from her hike. She went to the fridge and pulled out a bottle of water.

"I watched a documentary on culinary traditions the other night," she said. "They were interviewing a famous chef—though I forget his name now—but he said that these days it makes more sense for a chef or a restaurant to make their mark through concepts rather than signature dishes."

Carly perked up at that. "Really? Like, what do you mean?"

Neva shrugged. "I'm not exactly sure, but something about you create your own style so that eventually, someone only has to look at your dishes and will know who it came from."

"That sounds interesting," added Janie. "But again, I think that will come as you learn more about your cooking and creating strengths in school. Possibly not something you'd know right now."

"Fine," Carly said. "I'll stick to a specific dish for now. I'm thinking I'll perfect my own carrot curry and ginger soup with espelette croutons and pea shoots. But it's going to take a lot of practice."

"That's a mouthful," Neva said, then giggled. "Literally."

Janie had a feeling that the upcoming inn guests were going to be eating a lot of carrot soup with

Carly's spin on it. But it would be delicious, so it didn't matter.

Just the week before they'd had her salmon with sorrel sauce and Janie was still fantasizing about it. Her daughter was so talented in the kitchen. Now that the inn was doing better with the finances—and Carly was a huge reason for that—Neva was putting up a nice percentage of all the profits for the girls' education.

"Speaking of cooking, has anyone seen Ms. Baines since earlier today?" Neva asked.

"No, but I made her up a vegetarian pie with a filo pastry that comes in at under four hundred calories for the whole thing. The lentils will give her protein and the roasted vegetables are delicious," Carly said. "Let her know it's ready to pop in the oven when she wants to, and she'll have something hot to take to her room. I saw her nibbling on just a plate of celery and carrots last night for dinner. She has to be starving."

"You are such a good girl," Neva said.

Carly blushed. "She didn't ask me to do anything, but it's good practice. I hope she's not allergic to mushrooms. Honestly, I don't even think she needs to lose any weight. I mean—I'd love to have those curves and would trade her my skinny bones any day."

Janie laughed at that. "Oh, give it time and don't wish away that slender body of yours too soon, my girl."

Neva nodded in agreement. "Your mom is right. One day you'll dream of the days past when you could fit into anything off a store rack."

"Oh stop, Aunt Neva. You look amazing, and you know it," Carly teased. "I hope I get your genes. No offense, Mom." She gave Janie a guilty grin.

"No offense taken."

It was true. Neva was still quite fit, especially for her age. Janie wished she would take after her, too. But her own genes were proving to be a bit more robust. And with Carly's cooking lately, Janie dreaded to even guess how much weight she'd put on since moving to Linden Falls permanently.

Max would be surprised when they met for the final dissolution hearing.

"And what's on the menu for our other guests?" Neva asked.

"Pepper-stuffed tenderloin, maple-drizzled baby carrots and roasted potatoes," Carly said. "And I made enough of the zucchini cupcakes for their dessert."

Janie shook her head in amazement.

"I cannot wait," Neva said. "And Mr. Harmon will be here, too, so I'll tell Breeze to set an extra place at the table."

"I'll tell her," Janie said. "I'm going out there now to check on her."

She left Neva and Carly discussing the menu for the next day and slipped out the kitchen door, only to nearly trip over Breeze who sat on the top step now, clasping her arms around her knees while she still watched the ants.

"Have they made much progress?" Janie asked, sitting down beside her.

"Oh, they've already taken away the dragonfly carcass. Now they're working on carrying leaves."

"I wonder what they want leaves for?"

"They cut them up and arrange them around their nests, then fertilize them with their own poop to grow fungus for their food farm to feed the colony."

"Wow. Sorry I asked," Janie said.

Breeze turned and looked at Janie, her expression solemn. "Mom, can I ask you a question?"

"Sure can."

"Why don't you love Dad anymore?"

The question caused Janie to freeze—both thoughts and breathing.

When she and the girls had left Linden Falls and returned home for a few months, things had gone well for a while. But soon she and Max had slid back into their old routines, barely seeing each other and when they did, not really connecting. Max worked as an operations manager for a large events firm that puts on events all over the northeast. His specialty was company expos, but it took a lot of what was supposed to be his off time to wine and dine customers to keep their accounts. Then on the other side of it, he and his project manager had a team to manage. Their events for the most part appeared to be pulled off flawlessly, but no one saw the toll it took on those behind the scenes to make it look that way.

It wasn't long after their reunion that Max was telling her about the next "biggest event we've ever had to do" and was like a ghost through their home, getting in late and leaving early. While he was freaking out over getting things lined up for the Champlain County Fair—

which undoubtedly was not a company expo—calling on every favor he had in his pocket to snag the top performers he could find, Janie had found herself missing Linden Falls. The town she'd discovered she had roots in wouldn't stop calling to her, and she felt invisible to her husband, so she'd had to make a big decision.

When she'd told Max they were returning to Linden Falls, he hadn't said much. She informed him that once again, she wouldn't ask for any financial assistance, other than for him to help out when the girls needed something. Janie didn't want to make it worse than it was, and soon her new store would hopefully bring her a tidy sum each month. Not to mention, their living expenses were very small now that they were at the inn and didn't pay rent or utilities.

So far, the girls had seemed to understand and accept her explanation that she and Max had grown apart in interests and ways of life. That they'd always work hard to co-parent but wouldn't do it as a couple any longer. That they would be getting a divorce.

"I thought you were okay with our decision to live apart, Breeze? You know you'll get to spend part of your summers with Dad. And some of the holidays. You said you were excited to move here fulltime."

"You didn't answer my question." Breeze wasn't backing down.

"Well, I—I … I'm not sure how to answer that."

"Does that mean you still love him?"

Janie felt sweat pop up over her lip. "Breeze, it's complicated."

Her daughter stood and crossed her arms. "No, it's not. Just say you don't love him. If that's how you feel. Say it, Mom."

"Breeze, stop it. You aren't going to take that tone with me. And for your information, I'll always love your dad, as your father. He helped create you and Carly, the biggest gifts I'll ever have in my life. He will always have my gratitude for that."

"But you don't have romantic love for him anymore?"

"Lordy. Have you been watching the Bachelor again? I told you that's crap and I don't want you—"

"—no, Mom. I haven't. I know what romantic love is without watching a reality show. You don't want to have sex with Dad now, fine. But can't we all live together again?"

Janie stood. She was going to have to use her mom voice and not friend mode. "Okay, that's enough. I'm not discussing romance with you, and you sure aren't old enough to talk to your mother about her sex life. How about we give it a few years? And right now, I'm going to walk down to the square and gather some of the flowers from the Linden tree if you'd like to go with me. But leave this subject behind."

Carly was usually the dramatic one, so Janie was reeling at the attitude that her youngest was showing.

Breeze turned on her angry face. "No. I'll stay here. As a matter of fact, I'll go have a talk with my aunt. At least she doesn't treat me like a baby."

With that she turned on her heels and went back into the house, leaving Janie feeling like she'd just survived a sudden thunderstorm.

JANIE TRIED to clear the anxiety from her body as she took the short walk to the tree, struggling to hold a basket in one arm and the small step ladder in the other. It was always upsetting when one of her girls was unhappy, especially because she tried to shield them from every problem in the world.

And especially when it was her fault.

Why couldn't she be happy with Max, a man who had worked hard to be a partner in the big job of supporting their family? A man who had chosen her and accepted her, despite her many flaws and the emotional baggage she'd carried around for years because she'd been cheated out of a father.

Now here she was doing the same thing to her girls. Right now, they could be back home in the city, living their normal routine.

But Janie would be miserable.

She loved Linden Falls. Here she felt close to her roots—the ones she'd never known she had until less than a year before. And here, she was able to toss off the person her husband expected her to be—the career woman who dressed in the latest styles, teetered around in heels and juggled it all.

The interior designer with the magic touch.

In her new shop she was just Janie. A woman who was finally embracing the sensitive nature and deep intuitions she'd always squelched. She still loved design, in an everyday and fun kind of way, but within the small town and the comforting inn where her father was raised, she was becoming who she was supposed to be, or at least she was trying.

Each step toward unveiling that authentic piece of herself was making it easier to breathe. She couldn't give it up.

Max would probably laugh at her now. Laugh at how she dressed, her mystical shop, and all her homemade remedies that she was having the best time producing. He'd waltz in wearing his two-hundred-dollar slacks and fancy shoes, not a hair out of place or even a hint of a five o'clock shadow, tell her she was losing her mind and then take her girls back to the city.

Janie felt the skin on her arms pop up in goosebumps.

Losing her daughters was not an option.

She needed to get those divorce papers signed. They stated she had full custody and so far, Max hadn't questioned that. Taking care of two girls on his own would never be possible with his business life and his many social engagements. Janie hoped she never had to attend another *business dinner and drinks after* again.

Even so, she'd feel better when everything was finalized and stamped by the judge.

It was all so much to figure out. But right now, she needed to get to picking. The flowers on the Linden tree bloomed for just two weeks, and today she needed to pick the first crop, then quickly get them ready for the next step in the process. She would have to begin drying them out for storage because their fragrance and taste only peaked for a few days.

She approached the square where the tree stood majestically, waiting with all its flowered bounty for her to hurry and pluck. She couldn't wait to try the recipe she'd found to make medicinal Linden tea and tincture. She'd read all sorts of ways to use the tree's flowers to treat colds, the flu, and anxiety.

Suddenly a bird dived at her head. It came from behind so she couldn't see it, but she felt it and dropped the ladder and her basket, then covered her head and crouched as the bird came for one more round.

When Janie stood and looked around, the bird was gone.

Across the way she spotted the inn's new guest, Coco Baines, doing a power walk down the sidewalk, and trying her best not to make eye contact with anyone. She wore a grimace of pain as she moved, but it didn't falter her stride.

Janie picked up her basket and ladder again and approached the tree. After she opened the ladder and arranged it under a full area of flowers, she began picking the blooms and stuffing them into the pockets of the apron she'd borrowed from Neva.

There were a few wishes hanging around her, but Janie didn't look at them. Neva hadn't yet passed that duty on to her and it would be wrong to peek at someone's inner dreams. She kept her gaze on the petals.

"Hello, tree," she spoke softly to it as she worked. Since embracing the more intuitive side of herself, she'd realized that she felt a deep connection to trees. She could even feel a vibrational energy from them when she placed her hands on the bark, their town tree had the most active energy of any she'd felt so far. She hadn't believed in its magic at first, but now she knew there was something very special about it.

A breeze rose and Janie inhaled the scent of the small flowers. It was intoxicating, something close to honeysuckle, or maybe Jasmine. She popped a flower in her mouth and closed her eyes.

They were good. A floral-like taste. Sort of like the small, sweet asparagus you could get in the specialty section at high end health stores. It amazed her how many gifts nature offered to mankind if they only took the time to seek them out or opened their eyes to find those right in front of them.

Next year she'd learn how to make honey from the tree. Linden honey was highly sought after and would be a great addition to not only her shop, but also the inn gift store that they were planning to open soon. Even the Linden seeds could be made into a chocolate substitute, but she was getting ahead of herself. One small feat at a time, she told herself as she reached higher.

"Need some help there?"

She paused to look and saw Calvin Phelps, their town reporter on the sidewalk with a dog. A very round dog, as it was. Dachshund, she thought. Stuffed sausage, more accurately.

"Hi, Calvin. Thank you, but I'm fine. Looks like you have your hands full, too."

He smiled and the dog pulled at the leash. "My grandfather's down with gout and I promised him I'd try to help him with Orson."

Janie wanted to say that the grandfather probably should've asked months earlier. The dog was so overweight that even in the cool spring air it panted, struggling to breathe.

"Yeah, well. You know how it is. Grandpa eats like a cowboy, and I think he's been passing the beans and wieners down to Orson, too."

Janie smiled at the irony. Weenies for a weenie dog. Or at least that's what Breeze called them. Now her youngest would be sorry she hadn't come along. She loved all the dogs.

"Well, hopefully you can get Orson on track," Janie offered. She didn't want to be rude, but she needed to get back to picking. It would soon be time for her to return to the inn.

"I just wish I had more time," Calvin said. Orson stopped pulling and plopped down, his body folding around his back legs in a very unflattering way. "I'm working on something really important. We might end up losing that tree."

"What?" That got her attention. The Wishing tree? *Their beloved tree?*

Before Calvin could answer, a squirrel shot right down from the top of the tree, and directly across the path of Orson, nearly close enough for him to reach his tongue out and pat it on the head.

But it scampered away—and Orson was up surprisingly fast for his size and leapt off the sidewalk and into the road in a mad chase, in which Calvin had no choice but to follow because the leash was still looped around his hand.

He yelled out in alarm, startling Janie so much that she nearly fell off the ladder, grabbing it with both hands, but just as she started to settle the wobbling down, she heard the screech of tires.

Oh no.

Her heart in her throat, she turned to look, expecting to see the dog sprawled out in the street in front of a car.

It was worse.

So much worse.

Janie didn't climb down her ladder. She *jumped* from it, causing it to rattle loudly and fall into a metallic banging heap as she hit the ground, stumbled up from her knees that screamed out in pain, and ran to help.

CHAPTER 5

It could've been worse. At least Calvin was alert and talking, and though he lay on the street with his right leg at a very odd angle, right in front of a bumper that belonged to a shiny, black Passat, he was alive.

Quite alive, actually.

He seemed to be more concerned about the story he wanted to get back to researching than being still and assessing his injuries.

"You aren't moving an inch until a medical professional gets here," Coco Baines said, putting her hand on his chest to keep him still. She'd been the closest to him when it happened and was crouched over him.

Janie had never been at the scene of an accident before, and she was shaking from the fright it gave her. Or her trembling could be coming from shock—not only shock that a man nearly lost his life—but shock and unbelief at the twist of fate that would have it be *her husband* who had struck him.

Max.

In Linden Falls, of all places.

Coco was doing all the talking and Janie was glad for that. She didn't think it polite to scream at Max and ask him what the heck he was doing there while a man lay hurting and waiting on emergency services. That could wait.

"You." Coco pointed at Max. "Pull your car over to the side so there's a clear path to this man. And you'd better hope you have a legal driver's license."

Janie felt a pang of indignation. Of course, Max was legal. He also had a perfect record. He may have mowed down their town reporter, but surely everyone could see it was an accident. It was the squirrel's fault. She'd seen it all.

Max nodded at Coco's instructions, seemingly shocked into silence, too. He went and moved the car, then got out again and knelt beside Calvin.

So far neither Calvin or Coco, or the half dozen other townspeople who had gathered, knew that Janie and Max were related, much less even knew each other. Which might be another reason Janie couldn't find her tongue.

Janie had shaken off her paralysis and taken the task of chasing down Orson, who hadn't gone far. Within a couple minutes, she had him secured. Now, in her confusion of what to do or say, she was relegated to leash-holder and sympathy-nodding-inn-keeper-who-couldn't-speak.

Max wasn't paying her any attention. She knew he was mortified.

"Was he speeding?" Paige whispered to Janie. She'd been one of the first ones at Calvin's side once Janie came back with Orson.

"No, of course not." She wasn't intentionally defending him, but Max never sped. He drove like a grandpa. Janie was the one with the lead foot. "Calvin's dog gave chase to a squirrel and jerked him into the road. I don't think there was time for him to stop the car."

"Hopefully there were witnesses," Paige replied.

Coco was a witness. And probably a few more people. Janie was too, but once they found out that Max was her husband, no one would take her word for his innocence.

"We don't need witnesses," Calvin said, overhearing Paige. "It was so fast, there was no way he could stop. It's Orson's fault."

Janie felt a huge sigh of relief flutter away from her and she wanted to hug Calvin. Max looked at her quickly, and she saw her feelings mirrored in his eyes before he looked away.

"I'm really sorry," Max apologized yet again.

"Are you a tourist?" Paige asked. "Just in for the day?"

He shook his head. "I'm—well..I.."

"He's my husband," Janie said. It wouldn't do to lie

to the people she was trying to become friends with. That's all she needed to get her new business blacklisted from the locals.

They all looked from Max to Janie, then back again.

"Your husband?" Calvin finally asked. "I didn't even know you were married."

A hurt look ran across Max's eyes before he shuttered it.

Calvin wasn't the only one in town who would be surprised. Janie liked to keep her private life just that. *Private.* She was already dreading this making the rounds and she hoped it didn't find its way into the Linden Falls Gazette.

"We're separated," Janie added. "Amicably."

Not totally true, but she didn't want anyone spreading gossip that she was running from a bad situation. The only situation she'd run from was trying to find herself.

"Yes. We co-parent well," Max added, but only Janie caught the tiny inflection of sarcasm. "As a matter of fact, I'm here to visit our girls and save Janie the drive into the city."

"That's nice of you," Paige said.

Now Janie felt irritated. He was trying to make himself look like a hero when he knew good and well that the girls weren't even scheduled for a visit.

A van swerved in around and beside them and everyone stepped back to allow the two paramedics to get out and come close to Calvin. They bent down and as one started taking his vitals, the other was pelting questions. Coco, with Paige's help, stood by to give what information they could. Janie and Max watched.

When the Constable pulled up in his marked blue sedan, Max looked even more nervous.

"What's going on here?" Constable Pike said as soon as he threw the car in park and climbed out. He was already pulling his leather notepad from his pocket.

Calvin waved his hand in the air from his place on the cement. "I'm okay. A little busted up but nothing that can't be fixed with some plaster. My fault, too. I chased Orson out into the road and got clipped."

The constable didn't look pleased.

"By whom?"

All heads turned to Max.

"By my husband," Janie said. "He didn't have time to brake."

Max nodded solemnly. "I braked as soon as I saw him, but it was too late."

"Any witnesses to that?"

"I saw it," Coco Baines said. "That's exactly how it happened. The dog just missed being hit, too."

"I need your driver's license and registration," Constable Pike said to Max.

Max handed them over and Pike took them to his car, leaving Janie standing with her soon-to-be ex and wondering what else to say. Finally, she guided him a bit further from everyone else.

"What are you doing here?" she asked.

"Breeze called me."

"Already? That wasn't even enough time for you to

get here." Janie remembered Breeze stomping off in a huff literally half an hour earlier.

He looked at her questioningly. "What wasn't enough time? She called me last night and begged me to come. Said she needed to see me."

"So, this has been building up," Janie said, sighing long and loudly. "I should've seen this coming, and I wish she had talked to me about it. I guess she's not dealing well with the idea that our separation is permanent. I think she held out hope that we'd come back together as a family. I'll talk to her. You can go back."

He jerked back as though he'd been slapped.

"Nope—not going back. Not yet anyway. Breeze asked me to come and I'm going to prove to her that she and Carly are my priority."

Janie narrowed her eyes at him. "Since when? What are you up to, Max? Don't you have an event to organize?"

He lifted his chin and looked down his nose at her. "I take offense to that, Janie. When have I not been there for my daughters when they needed me?"

Janie was instantly sorry. Max was right. He was a great dad, and he spent what little free time he had, with them. It wasn't his fault that over the years, they had simply become different people than they were when they'd married. However, his fatherly gesture to drop everything and come running made her nervous.

"Did you get your papers signed?" she asked.

"No. Not yet. Did you?" he raised an eyebrow.

"Sure did," she lied. "Just make sure yours are ready by our court date."

"A lot can happen in thirty days."

"What are you trying to say?"

He smiled, showing his perfect teeth that made her always think about how un-perfect hers were. She hadn't had parents who could pay for braces, and she sure didn't want to wear them as an adult once she could afford them herself.

"Not trying to say anything."

Janie shook her head. He was up to something. She knew that look in his eyes. "You can go ahead to the inn and see the girls. I'll be there after I find out more about Calvin. And after I pick my flowers."

"I can help you," Max offered. "I have plenty of time, unless your cranky town cop is going to throw me in jail."

"It's Constable Pike. And he has every right to be cranky. You mowed over Calvin."

"Accidentally."

"Listen, you need to be back on the road before four if you want to miss the traffic."

The constable returned and handed Max back his identification. "You'll also need to alert your insurance company of this incident, in case Calvin decides to press charges."

Max smiled politely. "I'll alert them, though I doubt it'll come to that. As he has said himself, I'm not at fault."

"There will be an investigation before that is official," Pike said, then went to Calvin to take his statement.

Janie shook her head. "Don't worry about it. Calvin is a very nice man and would never try to gain from something that was his own fault. You can go ahead and get back to the city."

"Oh, no worries. I'm staying the night," Max said. "I called Neva after I talked to Breeze yesterday and she set me up in one of the rooms. Complimentary, even. She also promised me that Carly would blow my socks off with dinner tonight, and I'm looking forward to it."

Janie didn't trust herself to speak. Why Max was inserting himself in her place—and her new life—was beyond her. And it felt just weird.

She turned her back on him and returned just in time to watch the paramedics load Calvin onto a stretcher and put him in their van. He was trying to resist, but finally he crossed his arms and shut up. He let out a long, exasperated sigh.

"We'll take Orson to the inn," Janie called out. "Don't worry about him."

Coco still held the dog's leash as they all watched the doors to the van close and then Calvin being driven away.

JANIE PICKED the flowers fast and furious, not even taking the time to enjoy the process she'd looked so forward to. Coco had taken Calvin's dog on to the inn, but Max had stuck to her like glue. She tried to pretend she was calm and cool, but inside her head it was pure chaos as she tried to figure out how to get him back to the city stat.

Moving to Linden Falls was a way to simplify her life. And she didn't need Max coming in and complicating it again.

"Please let me get up there for that," Max said. He held the ladder and gazed up at her.

"No. I don't need you. Go to the inn and find Breeze. That's what you said you were here for."

"But I'd also like to spend time with you."

"Don't be ridiculous." She glanced down and regretted it immediately. He knew exactly how to use his deep brown eyes to look sad. That was how he'd snagged her in the first place after they'd gone on their first date, and she'd turned him down for a second.

The girls got their stubborn streaks from him.

Why did life have to be so complicated? Janie wished she could turn back time to when she and Max were young parents, their girls still little and enamored with their parents. Times when they'd had next to nothing, but they'd found things to do that were free and fun, too. Sometimes tough, especially financially, but they were still better times. Sure, as they'd gone through life and embraced the success of their careers, they'd been blessed beyond measure, affording luxuries that some only dream about. A beautiful house, nice cars, and even taking the girls on trips and staying in some of the nicest resorts money could buy.

But as they'd made more money, they'd bought more things, and owed more bills. It was a carousel that felt impossible to get off—until Janie had decided to search out where her birth father came from, and she'd landed in Linden Falls and discovered Neva, her link to her past.

She wouldn't allow Max to take the peace she'd found.

"I'm coming down," she said. "I need to get Calvin's dog sorted anyway. Myster and Charm will be very miffed at his presence, I'm sure. We'll get Breeze squared away so you are ready to hit the road tomorrow morning."

She climbed down and found herself trapped within Max's arms against the ladder.

"Myster and Charm?" Max asked.

"They're cats. Excuse me." Janie pushed his arm out of the way so she could escape, but not before her senses were tickled with the spicy scent of his usual cologne. He kept himself immaculately well-kept. Always. That was one thing she'd miss about having him around. She appreciated his commitment to his person. Even on the days when she walked around with no make-up, hair up in a messy bun, and wearing a frumpy tracksuit.

"I like your new style," Max said as he was folding up the ladder. "You look comfortable."

"Yours too. Did you order that outfit from the

lumberjack store?" The plaid shirt and hiking boots he wore with his creased jeans were obviously new.

He laughed at her comment. "Well, actually no. They're new but I grabbed them at the mall. I expected this to be the dress code of a town this small."

She raised her eyebrows. "I think you can leave the stereotypes at home next time. You'll find that there's a lot of variety in the kinds of people who live here." Then she wanted to stuff the words back in her mouth because they implied there would be a next time, and Janie hoped to lay down some boundaries. Linden Falls was all hers.

"I'll take the ladder," she said. "It won't fit in your car, so I'll meet you there."

He shook his head. "Nope. I'll walk you—and the ladder—home. My car is fine right where it is. Carly can come get it for me. She'll love having a chance to drive."

"It's less than a block."

He smiled. "I used to love the opportunity to just pull my mom's car into the driveway. A block would've been heaven."

He was so stubborn.

"So, tell me what you plan to do with the flowers you were picking from that tree," Max said as they walked.

"Lots of things. First, I'll put them in a dehydrator. Later they'll be used to make medicinal tea and a few other things." She snuck a peek to see if his expression changed. He'd never been one to try any home remedies.

"That's exciting."

"Oh, really?" Janie said, stretching out the two words with sarcasm.

"Yeah, really. I remember when Carly was a baby and came down with colic. You warmed up olive oil and rubbed it on her tummy and it did the trick. I'll never forget that first full night of sleep we got after that. I thought it was amazing that you knew that trick."

"I can't believe you remember that," Janie said. "Though it wasn't just olive oil. It was a concoction of ginger, chamomile, and a few other things mixed with it. I'd forgotten that."

She made a mental note to work on the recipe and think about offering it in her store. She'd seen several flustered tourists about town with fussy babies since she'd moved there.

"Yeah, and that time that I was mowing the lawn and stepped in a hornet's nest. You taught me to make a mud pack and then we ran to the store for tobacco to chew up and put on it. You were always coming up with stuff like that."

"Well, to be fair, everyone knows about mud and tobacco for stings. Since then, I've learned just a drop of undiluted lavender oil works even better than those."

She realized that she hadn't told Max about her store yet and while she'd at first thought he'd look down his nose at it, now she wasn't so sure. His remembering her home remedies from so long ago was a bit surprising.

They arrived at the inn and Janie led the way to the back and showed Max where to put the ladder, then took him in through the kitchen door.

Neva and the girls were there and when Carly and Breeze saw their dad, they screamed and ran to him to be enveloped in his arms.

Janie turned away.

"Neva, did you hear about what happened at the square?"

Neva nodded. "I sure did. Poor Calvin. And poor you, too, Max! I'm sure that gave you quite a fright."

The girls let him go. "It sure was. I feel just terrible about it, but I honestly didn't have time to stop. It was like he came out of nowhere."

"Where's Coco and Orson?" Janie said.

"Oh, I sent her on over to Calvin's house with Orson. He looked quite shaken, and I think he needed to go back to where he feels safe. I told Coco where to find the extra key and she said she was happy to stay until Calvin came back. She really is a nice person, down under all that anxiety she seems to carry around."

"Dad, I'm making your favorites for dinner," Carly said, changing the subject to herself as teens tended to do.

He smiled broadly. "Pepper-stuffed tenderloin, maple-drizzled baby carrots and roasted potatoes?"

Carly nodded. "Yep. With bacon-wrapped jalapenos on the side."

Janie knew then that Carly and Breeze were in it together. Her menu choice for dinner couldn't be that big of a coincidence. It had taken some planning.

Max grabbed his stomach and rolled his eyes back in his head. "I just have to let you know, you're in the running for favorite daughter."

"Dad!" Breeze exclaimed.

He laughed. "I said *in the running*, not the winner. I have yet to make my decision."

"That would be a hard one," Neva said.

Janie hid a smile. She'd heard the same exchange too many times to count. Max would never pick a favorite.

"What about school?" Max asked, suddenly serious. "Shouldn't you girls be doing homework?"

"Mine was done before ten this morning," Carly said.

"Breeze did hers early, too." Janie offered proudly. She was so proud of the girls for staying on top of their work. Home schooling really agreed with them.

"Well, great," Max said. "So, what can I do to help? If you're going to be in the kitchen, I'm going to be in the kitchen. Family time is precious. Wash up, Breeze. Carly is going to put us to work."

Janie crossed her arms over her chest. Max had never, ever helped in the kitchen.

Something smelled fishy.

CHAPTER 6

Coco felt weird sitting in a stranger's home, on a strange but comfortable sleek, leather couch, comforting a strangely overweight dog while she watched the clock. She'd agreed to bring Orson home because when Neva had asked her and placed such trust in Coco that she'd tell her where the key was to a man's home and allow her access without worry, the moment had felt good.

Her social life had been narrowed down so much in the last few years that she didn't have many friends, much less strangers, who would feel comfortable enough to hand over their dog and a key to their home.

Linden Falls was different on so many levels.

Orson approached her again, panting and giving her an intense gaze.

"If you're looking for a treat, don't come to me. You need to lose a few pounds. Well, I do, too, but I'm not coming at you with big puppy eyes and drool. So, the answer is no."

He put a paw up on her knee, his gaze unwavering. He let out a pitiful whine.

Coco sighed. "Oh, you're good."

She rose and went to the kitchen, then peeked in the pantry and found a bag of dog treats.

"One. Don't ask me again, either." She tossed it to him, and he missed it, but slobbered it up quickly from the floor.

The home was a historic one and though it appeared that the many original touches had been left, like the wainscoting and elaborate trim work over the doors and around the windows, the furniture and decorations were all more modern and quite nice. The floors appeared to be original hardwoods and they were scarred with character beneath the nice area rugs arranged about.

Coco assumed Calvin lived alone, as she didn't see evidence of anyone else but more than that, it just felt like a bachelor's home.

Respectfully, she'd stayed in the living room or kitchen, but now a few hours had gone by, and she was bored. After checking the front window again, she meandered down the hallway.

A series of at least two dozen frames held newspapers, all of them with Calvin's name at the byline. Coco remembered when she'd reported for a small-town paper. It was considered paying your dues, but she'd had her eyes set on progressing up the ladder from the very first day. It appeared that Calvin hadn't been as ambitious.

One specific headline stopped her in her tracks.

Linden Falls Woman Finds Her Backyard Tree Shedding Money

That one was interesting. She already knew about the famous tree for wishes but the town had a money tree, too? Someone had been drinking too much tequila, obviously.

She chuckled and moved on to read the rest of them. One reported that a Michelin-starred chef had moved to town. Another about a donation of a beautiful piece of art to the local library and yet another chronicled the adventures of a bear who broke into the local Curl & Dye beauty salon and how the owner, Vera, used her honey-infused shampoo to lure it out before it did any more damage.

On the opposite side of the hallway were framed articles about the town Wishing tree and the suspiciously magical results it had provided the locals and even tourists. Long lost loved ones reunited and the like. Coco liked the other side better, as she was a practical kind of girl and didn't give much credence to wishes.

Turning back around, she saw a photo of Neva, Janie, and the two girls in a story about an Italian-themed dinner gala at the Aspen Care Senior Center. Coco thought she could see a look of sadness hidden in

Neva's expression, but before she could think too much on it, she heard a car door.

She hurried back to the couch and settled next to Orson, hoping it wasn't too obvious that she was out of breath. She didn't want him thinking she'd been nosing around.

The door opened and there he was, his face surprisingly cheerful considering he was struggling through the archway on a pair of crutches, one leg in a gangly cast from mid-thigh to his ankle. The car that had dropped him off sped away.

Orson leapt off the couch and trotted over, his tail wagging at a faster pace than his chubby legs could move.

"Oh, gosh. Let me help you," Coco said, rushing to get up and go to him.

"I got it, I got it. Thanks."

But he didn't have it. When he reached to try to shut the door behind him, he lost his balance and would've fallen right on his face—or on top of Orson—if Coco hadn't grabbed him and supported his weight until he was stable again.

"Let's get you to the couch," she said. "Orson, move."

Funny how she already felt familiar with the dog after just a few hours.

"It's okay, boy." Calvin comforted him as he made his way to the living room, then settled down in the recliner next to the couch.

Coco took his crutches and propped them against

the wall, within reach. She stood back, rubbing her hands.

"I really didn't expect you to have such a serious injury," she said.

"I did. I was trying to be tough out on the street. The poor guy didn't mean to hit me, and it totally wasn't his fault. But I knew my leg was broken. Turns out it's a pretty bad break. A tibia-fibula fracture."

"No surgery?"

He shook his head. "For now, he doesn't think I'll need it. He set it before casting it, and I have to keep weight off for at least six weeks."

"Yikes. I'm so sorry." Coco stood there, feeling awkward. He hadn't asked her to sit down.

"Me too. But I was on crutches in high school once for a torn ACL and I got pretty good at getting around. Hopefully those skills will come back. If they don't and I continue to be a klutz, it's not going to be easy to do my job from this chair."

"You have a laptop though, right?"

He nodded. "I do, but in a town like this, in-person investigation and reporting are much preferred over emails and social network. I doubt half of our locals even know what Facebook is, and many of them don't even subscribe to the internet at all."

"Wow. I can't even imagine. I do most of my job via the internet," Coco said.

"Oh, what do you do?"

"Coincidentally, I'm also in broadcasting. So far

only field reporting and other jobs in the newsroom but when I go back, I'm going to be an on-air anchor." As soon as the white lie came out of her mouth, she felt guilty. She'd only get the job if she somehow proved herself physically and visually fit for it.

"Oh? That's great. Congratulations. What station?"

They talked a bit about her station and the highs and lows of the media arena, until conversation fizzled. She didn't mention her latest gripe with it.

"Well, I guess that's it, then."

"I'm sorry, I'm so embarrassed, but I didn't get your name," Calvin said.

"Oh—that's right. We weren't properly introduced. I'm Coco Baines, just a visitor to the town. I'm staying at the inn and as you know, I was there when you.. well, when.."

"When Orson pulled me out in front of a car." He smiled, then grimaced.

"Right. Well, okay, then. I guess I'll go. Do you need anything first?"

"As a matter of fact, I do. If you could go check my mailbox on the porch and see if my medicine has been dropped off yet, that would be great. It was supposed to beat me home, but in all the effort to get up the steps, I forgot to check."

"Sure. I'll be glad to." Coco went out to the porch and peeked in the mailbox. There was a small white bag stuffed inside it. She pulled it out and returned to the living room.

"It's here. Should I get you some water to take it with?" she assumed the prescription was for pain.

"Yes, please."

Coco went to the kitchen and poured a glass of water from the tap, then opened the bottle and shook out a capsule. She read the bottle quickly and saw that it said to take with food.

"You need to eat with this," she called out. "Do you have some crackers or something you want me to bring?"

"There's pudding cups in the fridge. One of those will do."

She returned to the living room with the pudding, water, and the pill. He took them and thanked her again.

Orson jumped up and went to the door.

"Whoops. I hadn't thought of what I'm going to do about Orson," Calvin said. "My grandfather had to move to the Aspen Senior Center, and I promised him I'd keep Orson."

"I'll take him out really quick," Coco said.

Orson followed her right out the back door, quickly did his business and then returned with her, settling himself in front of the recliner.

"Please sit down for a minute," Calvin invited. He had reclined his chair back and looked as comfortable as could be expected for someone with a broken leg.

Coco sat down on the couch. Orson looked up at her with broody eyes, willing her to say something. It was times like this that she wished she wasn't so proper.

"I can come and walk him a few times a day if that will help. At least for the next few weeks before I go back to the city."

Calvin looked ecstatic. "That would be wonderful. But are you sure? I hate to impose."

"It's fine. I'm not doing a whole lot of anything else while I'm here."

He looked suddenly interested. "So how much of your time here is supposed to be work-free? You wouldn't want to help me with a story I'm working on, would you? I'm sort of a one-man-show with the Gazette and I do it all. With my leg like this, I won't be able to get around and I'm going to need to take this pain medication at least for the first week. I'm pretty sensitive to drugs so I don't even know if I'll be able to write anything that makes sense," he paused and took a deep breath. "Now I sound like an idiot with all this babbling but I'm sort of in a bind here. The paper is kind of my baby."

"First, you don't sound like an idiot, but I'm not sure if I can help," she trailed off, not wanting to commit. Her attention span was short lately and she needed to concentrate on the goal she'd had in coming to town. "What's the story?" She expected him to come back with something small town and simple, like an elaborate upcoming wedding or a lost dog finds its way back, so she was surprised at his next words.

"I found out that we are going to lose our famous

Wishing tree. A sports bar chain bought the old King building at the square and the inspector said the plumbing is a disaster because the roots of the Wishing tree crept underground and grew into the pipes. The tree must come down and when the people of Linden Falls find out, there's going to be a lot of trouble. I'd like to break the story first and get reactions, but as you can see—I might need some help with the footwork. No pun intended."

Coco was a bit astonished. It was obvious that the Wishing tree on the town square was the highlight of the town and beloved by all she'd come across. It was a living, breathing thing to them.

"What does your tree warden say about it? He's going to let this happen?" she asked.

"Our city hall never appointed one."

She shook her head. "That's a problem then."

Coco knew from past stories she'd covered about trees and the fight to preserve them that many small towns and cities throughout Vermont still used an appointed tree warden, a practice that started more than a hundred years back in which the tree warden had full authorization over the decisions about trees that grew in public or private. The wardens are considered a voice for the trees and were implemented way back in the 1800s when Vermont had lost more than eighty percent of their forestry to the timber industry. With new guidelines in place and many rich landowners buying up acres of property to then donate to the state to be protected, the trees were back, but the practice of having tree wardens remained in effect.

"It sure is. From what I heard, the owner of the sports bar hired some fancy lawyer from Burlington, and they did everything on the sly. It's supposed to happen in less than a month, and I don't know what can be done, but we do need to get the story out there."

"You want the scoop," she said, a knowing smile creeping up.

He shrugged and looked embarrassed.

She felt sorry for him. She knew the fever of being the first one to scoop a story. Calvin wanted to be the one to tell it to his friends and neighbors before it got around the grapevine.

"It's not just about the scoop, though. I love that tree just as much as everyone else in Linden Falls does. I have a lot of fond memories attached to it. My grandfather used to take me to town every Sunday afternoon to get a sundae at Doc's Fountain. Then we'd sit by the tree and watch the people go by. Meet friends there. Talk to tourists. My grandfather would tell me stories about his own childhood and how he climbed the same branches that I liked to hang off. It was something else besides blood that connected us. Something we shared and no one could take away."

He looked melancholy. He hadn't talked about missing his grandfather or what sort of shape the man was in, but it was clear they had a bond.

She relented. "I tell you what, Calvin. You write the story tonight, and I'll come back in the morning to walk Orson. I'll bring some pictures of the tree, and I'll take the time to edit your piece before you run it. We'll get it done together."

"Thank you, Coco Baines. I don't know how you came to be in this town, but you sure have perfect timing."

With that she said her goodbyes and left, closing the door quietly behind her, then working up to a slow jog to get back to the inn.

CHAPTER 7

The next morning Janie woke before everyone else because she couldn't sleep and decided to just come on out to the kitchen and have some tea. It was only five o'clock so that meant she'd have an hour to herself—or with Charm and Myster, who were happy to have an early riser for company.

Charm moved gracefully in and around Janie's ankles and Myster watched her from the kitchen windowsill, his usual sly expression nearly comical. He always looked like he was up to something, and most of the time, he probably was. She looked down at her wrist, making sure she'd picked her bracelet up off the nightstand before Myster could sneak off with it. He was the only klepto-cat she'd ever heard of and if you didn't watch your stuff, he'd have it squirreled away.

Carefully she blended ginger, cinnamon, and licorice root at the bottom of her favorite mug, then poured boiling water over it. The combination of the three ingredients were perfect to help with anxiety or nervous tension, which were the culprits that had kept her awake most of the night.

She took the mug to the table and sat down. She blew across the surface of the golden liquid for a few seconds, then closed her eyes and brought it to her lips.

"Morning."

Janie nearly dropped the mug.

She turned to find Max standing there, already neat and put together.

"What the—"

He'd startled her. And surprised her. He hated getting up early.

"Sorry. Didn't mean to scare you. I couldn't sleep in today." He went to the coffee maker and finding his way, opened cabinets until he found the canister of coffee, then proceeded to prepare a pot.

"Headed out?" She hoped. She hoped. She hoped.

Janie was proud of herself for not bringing it up at dinner the night before. She'd respected that the girls wanted to have a nice meal with their father, without any friction. Then she'd even kept her mouth shut when they'd begged for him to sleep in their attic apartment. Against their protests, she'd taken the room that Neva had set aside for him. After she'd put all the flowers from the tree on liners and into the dehydrator, she had nothing else to do.

She'd gone to the room and lain awake aggravated because while she was lonely and bored, Max was cuddled on the couch with the girls, most likely watching Beauty and the Beast, or Mulan, and eating buttered popcorn. (she'd smelled the popcorn but was guessing at the movie)

"Nope. Not today," Max said, his tone cheerful.

"Oh?" Janie tried to play it off nonchalantly.

"Yeah, I'm taking the girls up to Magic Mountain after we drop my car off at the local body shop. Bud Hargraves said they have a loaner for me to drive while he pulls out the dent that your newspaper guy's leg put in the front quarter panel."

Janie cringed. "You know that Calvin's leg is broken, right?"

Max looked uncomfortable.

"I'm sorry," Janie volunteered. She didn't want to be mean. "It wasn't your fault. I'm just saying. But why don't you do that at home? Since it's mechanically safe, and I'm sure it's going to take some time to repair your bumper to perfection."

And by all means, Max was all about perfect. Which was why him hanging around was so weird. He rarely took off from work, unless it was a well-planned-in-advance family vacation, and even those were rare.

He shrugged. "He said a day or two. I told him that's fine. I'm not going to turn it in on insurance because it's minor and I don't want our rates to go up. He's going to cut me a deal just because he hates dealing with the insurance too."

"Oh. Yeah. About that, Max. I'm going to get my own auto policy soon. I just haven't thought about it with all the fuss in getting the new store started." She was embarrassed. He was paying her premiums and that wasn't fair.

His coffee was ready, and he poured a cup, then joined her at the table.

"Take your time. It's on autopay so it's not a big deal. And about your store, Janie. I know it's hard to fund a start-up and I can help out there, too."

She shook her head. "Thanks, but it's not really a start-up like in the big city. I don't have tons of capital in it yet. I'm buying a little of this and that, until I see what sells around here."

He stared at her across the table and for once, she couldn't read him.

"So, what did you and the girls watch last night?" she said, trying to move to safer ground.

"Mulan. It was Breeze's turn to pick."

Janie laughed. "I knew it. Well, it was either that or Beauty and the Beast. But I wasn't totally sure that Carly wouldn't try to throw something new and more mature out as an option. I know she's been all into some series on Netflix lately."

"Nope. She said she didn't mind. She snuggled in with us on the couch but was pretty occupied on her phone. Texting someone during the whole movie. I asked her to put it away once and she said she was looking up recipes, but I don't think so."

"That sounds about right. Could've been a local boy named Jonathon. But who knows, she's always making new friends online."

He scowled. "I don't like that."

"No, I make sure she's safe, Max. Don't go overboard. She's fine. We're all fine."

He scowled deeper.

Janie was tired and cranky. She didn't need his judgmental look. "What are you really doing here, Max?"

He took his time answering her, first taking a big drink of his coffee. "Are there any pastries in this kitchen?"

Her irritation flared but before she could say anything else, Coco Baines came in.

"Good morning," she said. "You both are up early."

She went to the coffee maker and poured a cup.

"Yep. Seems everyone is getting a jump on the day today," Janie said, the sarcasm heavy.

Coco leaned against the counter. "I told Calvin I'd come over early and take Orson out."

"That's so nice of you." Janie saw Max visibly cringe at Calvin's name again.

"He wants me to look at a story he's working on, too," Coco said.

Neva sauntered in, her feet in scruffy old pink slippers and wearing a very worn Chinese flower-embroidered housecoat. Her hair was up in a French twist, and she looked very much like the matriarch of the house she was. "The one about the new owners of the old King building wanting to take down the Wishing tree?"

"What? Why?" Janie said, feeling her stomach drop.

Coco's mouth dropped open. "Yes, that's what the

story was going to be. How did you already know that?"

Neva looked very upset. "It got around last night from one of the ladies at the widow's book club. She heard it from her cousin who is married to a man who works for the contractor coming down from Burlington to cut the pipes open. Word spread fast after that."

"Why would they want to take down that beautiful tree?" Max asked. "Isn't it the town landmark?"

"Unofficially it is," Janie said. "Neva, I'm so sorry. Is there anything that can be done about it?"

Neva shook her head sadly. "I don't know. It's related to an empty building across the way. A popular sports bar chain bought the old property and is going to have to take care of the water lines that've been a problem there for years. The inspection showed that it's worse than ever and they claim the tree's roots have crept under the street and into the pipes. The only way to find the exact problem area is to take the tree down and take up the sidewalk around it. Then they'll find the bad spots and then replace the pipes. Everyone is talking about it now."

"Oh no. Calvin is going to be so disappointed that word got out before he could break the news," Coco said. "I need to get over there."

Neva held a hand up to stop her. "You might want to wait until after the unofficial town meeting that's going to be at the tree at nine o'clock. Then you'll be able to give him more details for his story. The whole town should show up—no one wants to see that tree come down. It's the heart of Linden Falls and we aren't going to let it go without a fight."

"Good point. But I'll go by Calvin's first and touch base, then I'll get over to the meeting before it starts. Calvin may have some specific questions he wants me to ask. And I'm sure he'll want photos. We have a lot to talk about before nine." Coco put her cup down and hurried out.

Neva watched her go, then turned to Janie and Max.

"Well, now that I've got her bee in a bonnet, I'll leave you two at it and go back to my room to fix myself up a bit. I didn't know we'd have a gentleman up so early." She touched at her hair like a schoolgirl and grinned, then left.

Max nodded politely.

"Are you going to go to the meeting?" he asked Janie.

"I sure am. Neva loves that tree as if she gave birth to it and I can't fathom how she'll get over it if it comes down. Anyway, they're crazy if they think they can just waltz in and take down a historic tree like that when it's got plenty of living to do." Janie hadn't been a believer in the tree when she'd arrived in town the first time, but now she knew of too many serendipitous stories that had come true after hanging wishes on those ancient branches. And the tree was a living, breathing thing that didn't deserve to die!

"Well, I've been down this road before. I once managed an event that was set on private property, and the same situation happened with a neighbor's tree. I can tell you this, unless there are some strict tree bylaws in place, or the tree has an official historical confirmation attached, it's going to be hard to fight. If it's causing structural damage to a property, the owner of the property it is causing damage to has every right to have it brought down."

"That is not what I want to hear, Max." She peered over the rim of her mug at him.

"I'm sorry. It's the truth. But money talks, too. Let me get on the phone and see what else I can find out. See if there are any other avenues to explore."

She shook her head. "No. This isn't your town and isn't your fight. You go do what you were going to do today with the girls. I don't want people getting the wrong idea about you and what you can do to help."

He looked disappointed. "But I want to help."

"Max, with all due respect, we don't need it. Go home." Janie dropped her gaze and picked up her cup. She took it to the sink and set it down, then without looking back or saying another word, left him there.

Dissolving a marriage was hard.

No sense in stretching out the pain.

CHAPTER 8

Coco held the leash impatiently while waiting on Orson to find the perfect spot to do his morning business. Calvin was happy to see her, but she hadn't told him anything about what she'd learned, because she didn't want to make Orson wait any longer. They'd talk when she returned.

She'd hoped the dog would hurry but they'd already walked around the block once without success, and if he thought they were going for another round, he was mistaken.

Now they were at a standoff. "This is your last chance, Orson."

He tried to move another few feet, but she held the leash tightly. If she didn't set a boundary, they'd be going around the block all day.

Orson looked up at her, his eyes huge and sad.

Coco narrowed her eyes at him. "Don't even try. Just hurry up. I have a lot to tell Calvin about."

She saw an elderly woman and her tiny white Shih Tzu coming down the sidewalk at them. Orson obviously knew them, because he didn't bark, and the closer they got the more frantically his tail wagged.

The Shih Tzu looked equally as thrilled to see Orson.

"Good morning," Coco said.

"Morning," the woman replied, her face grim. She tried to keep her little dog from getting close to Orson, but the two stretched to the very end of their leashes, bound and determined to touch noses.

When the smaller pup flicked her tongue at Orson and nearly touched him, he got so excited that he instantly twirled and squatted, suddenly ready to do his business.

The smaller dog did the same.

The woman looked beyond disgusted and started fumbling for her plastic bag.

It was an awkward moment like Coco had never been in before. What do you say when your dog is pooping in sync with a dog of a grumpy stranger next to you?

"I guess they're pooping in solidarity," Coco offered.

No response. The woman looked over the dogs' heads as though studying a speck in the distance, her expression like stone.

"Which I guess is better than liquidarity." Coco laughed. "That would be a mess."

Nothing.

Coco was embarrassed but she also felt sorry for

the uptight woman who couldn't take a joke to lighten up an awkward moment.

Orson finished first and turned to his love interest to see if she was through as well. Coco held the leash firmly as she hurried and picked up his deposit, tied a knot in the bag, then pulled him along and back to the house.

"You need to choose someone from a different background, buddy. That one had a snooty mom, and you don't want to get into that family."

She was still talking Orson through his disappointment at not getting to romp and frolic with Suzy Shih Tzu when they entered the house.

Calvin was in a kitchen chair at the table, his hair still wet and his face clean shaven.

"How was the walk?"

"Okay, except we ran into a woman and her little white dog and Orson got overly enthusiastic."

"And the woman didn't, right?" he grinned.

"Right. She wasn't too happy for her dog to be cavorting anywhere near Orson."

"Don't pay her any mind. She's always crabby in the mornings but she warms up when the temperatures do. She misses my grandfather, I think. I know she used to bring him tomato biscuits and now she doesn't have anyone to hover over."

"Oh, that's sad. She must be lonely."

"Well, I told her she could go visit him. He'd love to have more company, but I think she's worried about what people would think. Here in the neighborhood, she could come and go without much notice, but at the center it would be much more obvious. Anyway, I was able to write up something last night. I want you to see what you think."

Coco took a seat opposite him. She wasn't looking forward to stealing his thunder.

"You may need to rewrite it no matter what I think. I'm sorry to tell you, but the news is already out."

He looked crestfallen. "Gosh darn it. I should've moved faster on it."

"Well, it's not like you could've done anything after being in the accident. Anyway, there's a town meeting this morning at nine o'clock. Ms. Cabot said just about everyone will be there. Are you going?"

He looked down at his cast. "I wish but there's no way. I'm much clumsier on the crutches than I expected to be. And my leg is really hurting. I hate to ask, but do you think you could go for me?"

"As a reporter?"

He raised his eyebrows imploringly. "Well, not officially. My editor won't pay you, if that's what you're asking. Actually, I'm still getting paid, and I can offer you something."

She laughed. "No—that wasn't what I meant. Do you want me to take notes?"

"I'd love that. Maybe I can edit what I already wrote and get a story sent in by deadline today. That would be so helpful, Coco."

Coco looked at her watch. "We still have an hour.

Would you like me to cook you some breakfast, seeing how you are feeling clumsy?"

She was joking and when he laughed, she was glad to see he had a sense of humor. Unlike the woman she'd seen earlier.

"I don't have much in there. As you can see, I'm a bachelor and I behave like one. But you're welcome to try. I mean, if you'll eat, too."

Coco didn't want to comment on the bachelor detail. Calvin was nice, but he was the epitome of a small-town-reporter, messy hair and spectacles to boot. While she was certainly no beauty queen, he was not her type, and she didn't want to encourage anything. Even if he had been her type, her life didn't have room for romance.

"We'll see. While I rummage around and get started, you fill me in on what you know about the background of the property that is going to be the downfall of the Wishing tree."

She got busy, pulling eggs and parmesan cheese from the fridge. She grabbed the tub of butter and in the pantry, found a can of sliced mushrooms. Calvin had a few tomatoes sitting on the windowsill and they were nearly too ripe but would be perfect for an omelet. While she cooked, he talked about the building.

"It was the town's first dry goods store back in 1854 and was owned by Vickory King, who was also the first Linden Falls postmaster. When he sold it, it was turned into a Coca Cola bottling plant and stayed that way for twenty years or more. When it was damaged in a big storm, the taxes fell into arrears and soon became city property. Over the years it's been used occasionally for events and rented out for art exhibits and craft fairs. It's pretty run down inside, to be honest."

Coco slid the omelet from the pan onto a platter, then cut a quarter of it off and transferred that part to a smaller plate. The toast popped up and she buttered one piece generously, and put it with the big portion of omelet, and took it to Calvin. Her piece was left dry, and she took it with her smaller plate and joined him at the table.

Orson was in begging position, and Coco ignored him.

"And no one noticed the plumbing issues before now?" she asked.

He took a big bite and groaned with delight. "This is great. Thank you. And no—up until now there hasn't been a need for a more serious inspection. It's been a while since the building was used, though."

"That's too bad. If the issues had been addressed earlier, the tree might've been saved. But I fully understand that a sports bar—or any public establishment, really—needs to have proper plumbing and clear water lines."

He nodded, his mouth full.

"Speaking of water," he said when he'd swallowed, "I really need a shower but I'm not sure how I'm going to do it without getting my cast wet. I'm going to have to do some engineering while you're away. That being said, I apologize for my unkempt state."

She grimaced. "They make a waterproof cast protector that you can order or get from a medical supply store, but for the first week or so, you may want to consider getting by with a sponge bath. I wouldn't want you to fall in the shower and break the other leg."

He finished the omelet and set his fork down. "I'll be fine."

"I'll tell you what," Coco said. "If you decide you're going to attempt a shower, please do it when someone can be here in case you fall. A friend or family member. Then at least they can call for help if needed. You do have more family here than just your grandfather, don't you?"

"Not family. My grandparents raised me when my teenage parents couldn't step up to the plate. Ironically, after I turned eighteen, they married and moved to Florida. I never really had a relationship with them. After my grandmother died, it has been just my grandfather and me for the last sixteen years. I've got an aunt and uncle, and some cousins, but they live in Michigan. What about you? Do you have a lot of close family members?"

Coco thought of her own parents. Her father was busy with his obsession with drones and was in several clubs and competitions. Her mother led a yoga class and did retired-lady-stuff like volunteering for dog rescue and leading a church women's group.

"They're in Virginia. I used to be close to my mom, but over the years she's gotten harder to deal with and only wants to keep pestering me about getting married and having children. So, I stick to our Sunday afternoon calls for the most part. I'm too busy to do much more than that anyway."

"But you're lucky. You got to grow up with a mom and dad. I always wondered what that would be like. My grandparents were great, but they were already too old to be raising a child. By the time I was a teenager, they were asleep by seven-thirty every night. Luckily, I was the nerdy type, or I'd have taken complete advantage of it."

"So, you never got into any teenage antics?" she asked.

"Not really. Heck, my grandparents were dressing me in sweater vests and teaching me to keep my shoes shiny by the time I was ten years old. I did everything I could to make them proud of me, always fearing they'd regret taking me in. I was captain of the chess team and all about the marching band. And don't ask me what I played. I enjoyed it but after high school I never touched it again. I dumped the sweater vests too."

Coco laughed. "Now you have me visualizing you carrying a huge tuba while wearing your grandpa's plaid cardigan. With matching socks."

He narrowed his eyes. "I'm not telling. Those days are behind me."

She wasn't so sure. While he may not wear sweater vests any more, he still exuded nerd vibes that were obvious from the first moment they'd met.

"It's funny. While I was in high school, I didn't mind not being a cool kid. I know I was different, but I had my small group of friends who were also that way, and we found fun to get into. Then when I got to college, being different wasn't really a big deal. And suddenly, I had girls interested in me. Even if it was only to help them get through the heavy workload, I made some long-term friendships from it, after they got to know me. Well, at least from the ones who weren't too shallow."

Coco's experience in high school and college was totally different and now she wondered if maybe the nerdy-type kids had it better than she did. While she was obsessing about wearing the trendiest clothes and going to the right parties to conform and be considered popular, people like Calvin were doing whatever it was they wanted to, without the stress of trying to fit in. Coco was embarrassed now to think of how she thought her life would be over if she didn't get into the college house she wanted.

She got it and hadn't heard from one of her sorority sisters in nearly a decade.

Orson whined, breaking the moment.

"Do you think he needs to go outside again?" Coco asked.

"He might. Either that or he's mad that he didn't get his own omelet."

"Don't think I didn't notice you sneaking him some." Coco looked at her watch and then Orson. "Fine. I'll take you again but this time you'd better make quick work of it so I can get down to the square."

CHAPTER 9

*J*anie waited for Neva to finish getting ready and together, they went to the square. She thought they'd be earlier than most but when they arrived, there was already a crowd and the voices buzzed together like a swarm of bees ready for attack. Mayor O'Brien was in the center, next to the tree, and despite the morning chill he was sweating profusely.

And the tree.

Wow.

"Will you look at that," Neva said, then whistled low.

"I've never seen anything like it," Janie replied.

The tree wore—yes, *wore*—a beautifully crocheted sweater of many colors, fitted snugly against the trunk and climbing all the way up to where the branches stretched out wide like a lover's arms.

Judging by the Cheshire cat smile that Norma

Braxton and the other ladies of the Winey Widows wore as they flanked the tree, they were responsible for the endeavor.

"They must've stayed up all night creating that," Neva said. "I'll bet it was Jean's idea. When she was young, she was an activist. Or could've been Cecelia. She's quiet but has a stubborn streak a mile wide. Couldn't have been Norma's idea. She's much too busy helping coordinate the high school reunion coming up."

Janie smiled at Neva's contemplation. "It's nice but I don't think a sweater is going to protect the tree from coming down."

"Don't tell them that." Neva continued. "I'm going to join them up closer so I can hear everything."

"I'll stay back here." Janie hadn't been in Linden Falls long enough to really have any clout or to be considered one of them. And she preferred to be a spectator, though she'd do anything she could to help.

The book club ladies were on top of it, though. They all seemed to be speaking at once to the poor mayor.

He kept nodding his head, but his expression was one of confusion and a little panic.

Janie watched as more of the townspeople arrived.

Paige was there with Gladys, the town dog. Reed, her fiancé, was also with them. Paige's brother, Jed, and his family, including the two adorable children, walked up and was greeted by Walt and Leona Mills, who used to own the cabins at the edge of town. One of their renters, Jack Darby, fell in love with a famous English chef that came to Linden Falls for a visit. She fell in love back and since Walt and Leo were tired of living so far out, and ready to enjoy their retirement more, they sold them the farm and moved to town.

"Oh, how quaint. The tree is wearing a jumper," Verity, the famed English chef exclaimed, her lovely lilting English accent turning more than a few heads. Jack looked at her with a twinkle of love-infused amusement, and Janie felt a twinge of envy.

She looked away from their obvious infatuation with each other and saw that Brian and Barb McVey were there, and Barb looked close to tears. Faith from the Aspen Grove Senior center comforted her.

Eddie Preachers, the town coroner, stood a bit away from the crowd, looking as morose and bored as his job description called for. She wondered if he ever found reason to smile.

Janie watched as Susan Wilbanks and her partner in crime, Daisy Crawford, approached the mayor and the ladies. Their body language didn't bode well, and that was unfortunate because they were both on the town council.

"I don't know what all the fuss is about," she heard Susan exclaim. "We need that sports bar here so we can draw out the younger crowd. This whole town acts like it's in a coma when the sun goes down. It's ridiculous. The tree doesn't make money and is only a hindrance to bringing in revenue."

Daisy nodded in agreement, looking like a clueless bobblehead.

"You already got your fancy Linden Falls Fitness center. Why can't you leave well enough alone? We don't want our town getting all fancy and we sure don't need a bunch of drunks screaming at touchdowns and stumbling through town," said Cecelia of the Winey Widows.

"Hey—we all needed that gym," said Brian McVey, looking offended.

"Okay, let's not get ahead of ourselves and start attacking each other," Neva said. "The gym has been a blessing to many of us here. Not me, particularly, but others for sure."

"Oh, I'm sorry, Barb," Cecelia immediately apologized to Brian's wife.

Janie saw Daisy roll her eyes.

She'd better not be rolling her eyes at Neva. Janie wasn't too fond of Daisy, anyway. She'd fired Mary May from being her housekeeper just because Mary messed up and tried on one of Daisy's fancy dresses and a pair of her five-hundred-dollar shoes.

Then Daisy had tried to make a pariah out of Mary, only to have it backfire in her face and then in perfectly orchestrated karma, lost her own best friend to Mary May.

Jodi Snyder was that best friend and Janie saw her there, too, standing as far from Daisy as she could get. Jodi watched the street, probably looking for Mary to come be her support. According to what Janie had heard, Jodi had tried to keep up with the Jones'—or more accurately, the Wilbanks—for a long time before realizing that the stress of it outweighed the benefits. She seemed much happier now when Janie saw her around town. She was friendlier and comfortable in her own skin, despite it no longer being covered in the most expensive fashions.

And Mary May—whom Janie didn't see anywhere—now, she was an interesting sort. She'd been the recipient of some strange happenings, and no longer needed to clean anyone's toilets to stay afloat. Mary had lost her husband to philandering, but Janie heard that now she and Phil Steele, who owned the flower shop but was doing attorney work again, were an item.

According to Neva, Phil was depressed for years after his wife, Bertie, died. He'd struggled to keep her flower shop going and now Mary was helping him because she had a natural touch with doing the arrangements. *And with doing something else, obviously.*

Janie almost felt ashamed of herself, playing innocent bystander as the gossip ran through her head. You'd think she'd lived there forever, but it was surreal how fast the grapevine worked in small towns, whether you wanted to hear things or not. Things like how Daisy Crawford had to clean her own house now because her reputation went far outside the city limits, and she couldn't find anyone to take Mary's job.

Not that Janie would ever repeat any of it. But it sure was fun hearing it.

She saw Henry Harmon arrive with his regal black

cat, Mina, following him like a dedicated puppy. It was the strangest thing, but that cat went everywhere with him. It even sat outside the grocery mart when he went in to do his shopping. How it avoided getting run over, she couldn't guess. But obviously, the old myth was true, and cats were smarter than dogs, judging by the antics of the dog that got Calvin clobbered by Max.

Neva's face lit up at the sight of Henry as he moved in to stand beside her. Mina went to the tree and began sharpening her claws on its trunk, oblivious to the crowd who watched her.

"Hi Janie."

Janie saw Nicole, the waitress from the Crooked Porch, approaching. She was wearing her black pants and black shirt, a crisp white apron tied around her waist.

"Hi Nicole. Are you working?"

She looked sad. "Yep. But I had to slip out and see what's going on. I can't believe they want to take our tree down. It was here long before I was even born and even before my mama. I can't imagine this square without it."

"Hopefully they can figure out something."

A car pulled up and man in a suit stepped out. Janie didn't recognize him. He shook hands with Mayor O'Brien, who seemed relieved at his arrival. Around them the chatter still went on, with Susan picking at people about their sentimental feelings.

"Have I missed anything?"

Janie saw Coco approaching and waved her closer.

"No. I think they are about to start."

Coco pulled a notepad and pen from her bag and was poised to write.

Sure enough, the mayor raised his hands and slowly, the talking died down.

"This is Edward Applegate from the department of water management. He's going to explain what is going on and answer any questions."

Applegate opened his speech with a much-too-detailed report of how the tree's roots had over the years spread further and further until they'd reached the pipes that ran out from the old King building and finally, infiltrated and caused irreparable damage.

"There must be some other way," Henry Harmon said. "This tree has been the catalyst to a lot of wonderful things that have happened to the people of this town. There must be another option."

The mayor sighed and threw his hands up in frustration. "That's what he's trying to tell you. The new owner of the King building hired a private company to investigate and there's really no alternative. They'll dig down and follow the roots until we find the problem, then cut them out. And if we don't take the tree down at the same time, the roots will just do the same thing by this time next year."

"Not only that," Applegate said, "But a lot of the branches are at high risk of breaking off and hitting a car, or even a pedestrian. It could cost the town thousands of dollars or more if someone wanted to sue."

"I'm sorry but that's just ridiculous and has never

happened in the history of this town," Neva said. "She may lose some branches occasionally but never have they hit someone. Our tree has better manners than that."

Applegate looked confused.

"This is a historical tree. Think of all the wishes it has granted. You can't touch it," Coco offered up. "Isn't there a historical preservation committee here?"

The mayor shook his head. "I'm sorry, I don't know who you are but unfortunately, that's not a valid argument. This tree is not on our historical register and therefore is not protected. Also, whether the granted wishes are fact or fantasy cannot be validated."

Janie could almost swear she felt the whole town sigh in defeat.

"I don't care. She should be on the register, and I think we should put it up to a public vote," Norma said. "We should all have a say in something so important to the town as a whole."

"It's private property, so it's not the town's decision," Susan Wilbanks said. Her husband, Bob, had arrived and nodded his head obediently as he stood beside her.

"And the sports bar will be a great attraction for tourist season. It will bring in more capital to everyone," Bob said.

"Oh, why don't both of you take your emissions-nightmare of a Range Rover and go home," someone from the crowd said.

Susan looked around furiously, trying to figure out who said it.

"Quiet, please," the mayor said, his hands in the air like he was conducting a symphony. "Susan's right. It's private property and the owner has a right to decide what to do with his own investment."

"I just don't see how it's part of the King building's property," Walt said.

The mayor reached behind him and pulled a rolled-up document from his waistband. "Well, it is. I pulled the property plat to make sure. It's all right here and legal."

Sadder than the thought of losing the town's tree were the looks across the faces of those who loved it. The murmurs that went through the crowd sounded defeated and Janie felt like her heart was breaking for all of them, especially Neva who looked physically ill. Her aunt wasn't one to argue, but Janie couldn't believe she wasn't speaking up more.

"Where's the new owner? We want to talk to him," said Paige from the Townsquare bookstore. "My mom would roll over in her grave if she knew this was happening. Let's let him tell us how important his sports bar will be that we should lose a vital part of our town."

"The owner has asked to remain anonymous," said Applegate.

"He was invited here today, though," the mayor added.

Janie couldn't blame the guy. He probably thought

he'd be run out of town, and he was probably right. He'd stirred up a lot of bad energy and she pitied anyone who showed themselves as the instigator.

"You should've insisted he come, Jessie O'Brien. And don't go all official on me. Don't forget, I've seen you hanging by your underwear when you got caught in the barbed wire after sneaking into the Johnson's orchard to steal apples. You can do something here and you'd better do it," Neva said, the desperation ringing out for all to hear.

There you go, Neva. Speak up. Janie wanted to cheer aloud.

The mayor wrung his hands and bright red spots popped up on his cheeks. He looked like a scolded boy. "Neva, I'm sorry. I really am. I'm just as upset as you are, but the law is the law. We can't keep someone from doing what they need to do on their own property to protect their investment."

"This is not going how I'd hoped it would," Coco whispered to Janie.

Janie would've said something back but at that moment, she saw her aunt reach up and brush a tear from her face. Seeing Neva so upset just gutted her and she felt her own throat thick with tears. Henry put his arm around her shoulders and Neva huddled in.

Janie bowed her head, hoping no one would see her get emotional.

The mayor was peppered with a few more questions and ideas, but all were quickly shot down.

"Listen, that's all I can tell you for now," he said.

"The only other thing I want to suggest is that we have a celebration of the tree event before its final day comes. Maybe balloons? Fireworks? I'm open to suggestions, as long as it's not something extravagant. You can email them to me. For today, I'm done."

"You want to celebrate the death of our town tree?" someone called out.

"Wait a minute, I have something to say."

Janie's head jerked at the familiar voice, and saw that yes, it was Max approaching the mayor. What was he doing there and what in the world could he have to say?

She saw Breeze and Carly follow him to where the mayor stood.

"Who are you?" Mayor O'Brien asked.

"I'm Max Stallard, married to Janie who is Neva Cabot's niece, and I'm the guy that accidentally ran over your town reporter."

More whispers and Janie felt her face get hot. She didn't dare look at anyone else.

Max continued. "Sorry about that. But I'm also the guy who has been on the phone for the last two hours trying to figure out a way both your investor and the townspeople can be happy."

Everyone went silent, and Neva looked hopeful.

Janie was mortified.

"It's a new technology called cured-in-place pipeline, or CIPP and it's already being used in bigger cities like Toronto," Max said.

"The mayor and I have already discussed that technique," Applegate replied, looking nervous.

"It's a monumentally expensive method and the investor won't pay for it," the mayor said.

"Then the city needs to pay!" Barb said.

"I agree," called out Norma. "If it will save our tree, we need to do it."

"We don't have that kind of money," the mayor argued. "Nowhere near that kind, especially for something so complicated that's not a sure bet. You've all seen our annual budget. We're maxed out. You know we've been using the same holiday decorations for far too long, and last year we had to resurface the basketball floor in our high school. That was an unplanned expenditure, and it has our coffers low. There's no extra money for something like this."

"At least let him tell us about it," Barb's husband said. "It won't hurt to listen."

"Yeah, let my dad talk," Breeze called out. "What happened to free speech?"

Janie wasn't happy that Max was dragging the girls into a problem that would probably not be solved in the way they'd all like. She hated for them to be disappointed at the conclusion.

Max stood taller. "It is a very tricky procedure; I'll give it that. And it is expensive, but it could save the tree. A liner is inserted or pulled into the plumbing pipes that need repair, then the resin of the liner will cure and adhere to the walls of the old pipe to form a new one. The best thing about it is that it requires very little digging."

Another murmur rose in the crowd and the mayor held his hands up again. "Again, yes, this could've been a possibility but there is no money in our budget earmarked for this, and not enough time to raise it. I didn't even have to show up here today because the investor doesn't owe us an explanation, nor a consideration for recourse. Nothing short of a miracle is going to save the town tree and that's the bottom line. So, if any of you are handing out miracles, let me know but for now, this meeting is over."

He walked away to the chorus of grumbles.

"I've got to get back over to Calvin's house," Coco mumbled and took off.

Janie made a beeline for Max and her daughters. "Girls, let me and your dad have a talk, please. You go look around in the bookstore. I think Paige has free apple cider today."

Carly gave her a knowing look but obediently ushered Breeze down the sidewalk toward the store.

Max looked ready for her, his arms crossed and the stubborn expression she hated already in place. "I did it for the girls," he said before she could get anything out.

"I don't know what you think you are doing, Max, but I don't like it. You obviously want to be the hero. To the girls. Jeez—to the whole town. News flash, but you don't live here." She said, trying to keep her voice low, since Neva and a few of her friends were still at the tree. "And I know you. By tomorrow you'll have an urgent meeting to attend or a new event to bid for, and you'll be out of here. Then they'll all be looking at me like I'm the one to let them down."

"No one else had a viable idea, did they? At least I offered up something."

"Something that can't happen! This town isn't like the cities you work in, Max. It doesn't have big budgets to do things with. You heard the mayor. All you did was give them false hope." She lowered her voice. "Neva is crushed by all this, and your bright idea will only drag out the pain."

Max shook his head sadly. "Hope is the key word here, Janie. And they say a person needs just three things to be truly happy in this world: someone to love, something to do, and something to hope for."

She stared at him. He wasn't usually poetic with words, and she didn't know what to say.

He smiled gently. "I'll see you tonight at the inn. Unless you want to join us skiing?"

Janie turned and left him standing there, but not before she saw Neva tying a note with ribbon to the tree.

CHAPTER 10

Coco leaned back on Calvin's couch and crossed her ankles on the ottoman. Her laptop balanced easily—too easily, actually—on her stomach and allowed her to keep typing.

"What about this? The Linden Falls Wishing tree goes back to the days when—"

Orson chose that moment to try to jump onto the couch beside her. He missed and slid down the front of it like the Wiley Coyote in a cartoon, but he jostled her enough that she almost lost her laptop.

She set it aside and lifted him up. "Come here, Chubs."

He settled in right next to her, so close you couldn't put a butter knife between them. They had walked again, this time around the block not once but twice, as Calvin told her the little fellow was full of pent-up anxiety, and she wanted him to chill out while they worked on a piece to submit to the editor.

Calvin looked antsy from where he sat on his recliner, his frustration at being immobile coming through, but he had looked happy that Coco hurried back and filled him in on what happened at the meeting. So much so that when he'd asked her to stay and help him put something together, she hadn't the heart to say no.

"Okay. Let me start again," she said. *"The Linden Falls Wishing tree goes back to the days when the main street was laid with cobblestones and traveled by horse and buggy, the townspeople visited wooden storefronts to fill their pantries, and the tree's limbs and leaves were whipped about in slight breezes and hefty hurricanes."*

"I love it," Calvin said, his head bobbing up and down in approval.

"That's all I've got. Now what?"

"We need to talk about ways to raise the funds to do the CIPP."

Coco sighed loudly. "But we don't have time to raise funds. Not unless anyone who has any money in Linden Falls wants to write a big check really quick."

"I doubt that's going to happen. Anyone from here who has that kind of disposable money isn't going to give it away, or they would've offered at the meeting this morning."

"Good point." Coco wasn't sure why she felt so passionate about the tree. Even when she'd hung a wish on it, she'd really done so just to be able to tell Breeze she'd done so. She didn't believe a tree of any kind had any sort of power to change lives.

"We need to find something really important about the tree. I know he said that it's not on the town's historical register, but what if that's an oversight? Maybe there is something interesting that happened there."

Coco could see where he was going, and she liked it. "I saw the library when I drove in. How about I go there and see what I can find?"

"It can't hurt." Calvin looked hopeful. "I wish I could go with you, but the library is pretty small, and I think I'd probably upset our town librarian by making too much racket just trying to get around on these crutches."

"I tell you what. You stay here and make a list of the oldest Linden Falls residents and start calling them to tap into their furthest memories that have to do with the tree. I'll hit the microfiche and pull up old newspaper articles."

"I'll get right on it," he said, then flinched.

"Have you taken your pain medication yet today?"

His look told her everything.

She stood. "I'll take the pudgy boy out again and then come back and make both of us some lunch before I go. Then you take something for pain and have a nap. You can dig after that."

"No—I can't let—"

"You can and you will. I'll also throw some laundry in, and it can be washing while I'm gone. I'll dry it when I get back. Don't touch anything."

He leaned back with an exasperated sigh, but Coco could see he was relieved.

She beckoned at the dog. "Come on, Orson. And I hope we don't see Suzy Shih Tzu and her crabby mom out for a mid-day stroll because we don't have time for your butt-sniffing and her cold shoulder."

FOUR HOURS later Coco was out of breath by the time she half walked, and half jogged back to Calvin's house. She gave a few short knocks, and when he didn't answer, she opened the back door and peeked in.

"Calvin," she called out. When he didn't reply, she moved through the kitchen and tip-toed into the living room. The sight that met her looked like a Norman Rockwell painting for the modern day.

Calvin was stretched out on the couch. Orson was squeezed onto a space beside him, too small for his chunky self, and one of his hind legs dangled off the side. Calvin had one arm thrown over his face and the other resting on his open laptop.

She felt pity stir through her. Calvin had insisted he didn't want to take pain medication and now she knew why. It obviously knocked him out. As for Orson, he was a victim of his overwhelming fat to muscle ratio and his body would go into hibernation mode whenever it could snatch a chance.

"You're such a great guard dog, Orson," Coco whispered.

She wasn't sure how long Calvin had been sleeping so she decided to let him snooze a bit longer. Quietly, she made her way around the house, picking up discarded socks, and the dishes next to the recliner. She went to the laundry room and pulled the wet clothes from the washing machine and started them in the dryer.

Then after some consideration whether he'd be offended or not, she walked down the hall to find Calvin's bedroom.

Just as she suspected, it was a mess.

Working quickly, she pulled the rumpled bed clothes off and took them to the laundry room and started them washing. She found the linen closet and picked out a frayed blue set of sheets and put them on the bed, added the comforter, then did a turn down that would rival the Four Seasons.

Calvin lived alone and didn't have anyone to fuss over him while he was down and out. At least tonight he'd feel catered to.

While she was on a roll, she did a quick clean up in the bathroom, giving the toilet a swirl with the brush and rinsing the toothpaste from the sides of the sink. She didn't want to take on the shower after seeing how it would need some extra elbow power, but she grabbed the dirty towels and hurried to toss them in with the sheets.

Orson showed up just as she closed the lid to the

washing machine, his tail wagging, so Coco fixed his dinner and then waited on him to scarf it down before grabbing a leash and taking him out.

They did a super-fast power walk around the block, and when they returned both were out of breath, but she felt invigorated from the slight chill the evening was bringing on.

She peeked in and saw that Calvin hadn't moved an inch. It worried her.

"Wow," she said to Orson. "Should we check his pulse?"

He looked concerned that she looked concerned, and she crept over to the couch and held her hand over Calvin's face. When she felt his hot breath, she released a sigh of relief and returned to the kitchen, Orson on her heels.

By the time she'd opened a can of tomato soup and heated it, then divided it between two bowls and whipped up some grilled cheese sandwiches, she heard Calvin stirring.

"Stop it, Orson. I'm awake."

She smiled. Orson knew there was food coming and he was going to make sure Calvin was awake to give him a bite.

After she found a tray on the top of the fridge collecting dust, she rinsed it off and added a nice dishtowel to the top, then set the soup and sandwich on it with a glass of milk and carried it into the living room.

"Coco. I didn't know you were here," Calvin said.

He was sitting up. Immediately he reached up and tried to smooth his hair down but missed the cowlick that stood at attention in the front.

She brought the tray to the side table next to the recliner and set it down. Orson sniffed at it, and she gently swatted him away.

"Well, I am. Let's get you over here where you can get a bite to eat."

"Wow. I—I don't know what to say." He looked embarrassed.

"Thank you? Yum, I love grilled cheese? Either will do. Just hurry before it gets cold. I made some for me too and I'll tell you what I found while we eat."

He grabbed for his crutches and struggled upright. "I'll be right back."

Coco returned to the kitchen and set her own bowl on a large platter, added the sandwich, and returned to the living room. When she sat down, she realized that she'd forgotten, she wasn't eating cheese. Cheese and hips didn't do well together.

Oh, heck with it.

She dipped her sandwich into the soup and took a big bite, then closed her eyes with ecstasy. How could anyone ever really give up cheese?

Her sandwich was half gone by the time Calvin made his way back and settled himself into the chair. He was wearing a clean t-shirt and his hair was a bit damp looking. The cowlick was laying down, in wait for a dry spell to stand at attention again.

She pretended not to notice.

"You cleaned my bathroom," he said.

"Clean is a big word. Straightened is more accurate." She took a spoonful of the tomato soup. She wasn't going to mention his laundry, nor the streaks of toothpaste in his sink. "I'm definitely not a qualified housekeeper but I know how to make things look presentable."

"Do you live alone?" He asked, then started eating.

She nodded. "Yep. Just me. Thought about getting a cat after my last break-up but I work too much."

"Cats are supposed to be good for people like that. They aren't as needy as, say, 'ole Orson here."

"Yeah, that's what they say. But even for a cat, it would be a lonely life in my apartment. I tend to say yes to every little thing they need at work. I fill in for vacations and take all the crappy holiday schedules. All in my efforts to one day attain my dream position. Which looks like has all been for naught."

"Do you want to talk about it?"

She gave a small laugh. "No—not at all. I need to fill you in on what I found out. Did you know that in 1927, just a few years after women won the right to vote, three women hiked the Long Trail from end to end? They made history and I found an article and photo from where they made a pit stop right here in Linden Falls! And hung a wish on our tree. Oh—I mean your tree. They were the first women to complete the trail from end-to-end."

"Wow. That's amazing. Right here in Linden Falls, you don't say?"

"Sure did. Right in the middle of the silent movie era. Flapper skirts, bathtub gin. Can you imagine what the menfolk thought about it at that time? How much resistance they probably had to take?"

"I've got to see what these women look like. Wish I could meet them too," Calvin said. "Did it mention what their wish was?"

Coco swallowed her last bite of her sandwich, then retrieved her bag and pulled out her laptop. "No, it didn't. Burlington Free Press ran the story I found. It called them the Three Musketeers. In the photo they wore scarves on their heads, flannel shirts and fourteen-inch-high laced boots. They were serious about their endeavor. I read that they had to cross an old railroad trestle that was sixty feet in the air, over a dry stream of big boulders. They crawled across on the rotting timbers on their stomachs while balancing their packs on their backs, a few inches at a time. It said the trestle was so old the timbers were crumbling beneath their hands while they crawled. But they finished the trail in just thirty days."

When she stopped talking, she noticed Calvin wasn't eating. He was smiling at her.

"What?"

"You must love research. You are just lighting up while talking about it."

"What I love is that they discarded the stereotypical

position they were supposed to be happy in, donned men's clothes, and decided to do something no other women had ever done. They were brave." She turned her laptop around and showed him the photo.

"They sure set an example for women's rights, didn't they?"

Coco let out a sigh of frustration. "They did and look where we still are today. Women are still struggling to fit a certain look for everything they want to do. In media they must be slim and beautiful, plus whip smart and ambitious to boot. I've even known some networks to insist that their female anchors wear dresses while on air. It's like we are still living in the old times."

"That's just not right. I'm sorry, Coco."

She waved her hand in the air. "Oh, don't worry about me. Let's keep going. You know how Neva has a room dedicated to Robert Frost in her inn?"

He nodded.

She grinned slyly. "Well, he may have really stayed there. I found a reference to an inn in this area, that he says he frequented often and was the place he wrote a poem, get this—called *Wishes*."

Calvin's eyebrows raised up dramatically.

"And it's about trees!" she added.

"Seriously? I never knew that. Surely if we could prove it's our inn and the poem was inspired by our Wishing tree, that combined with the appearance of the Three Musketeers who made history for women's rights, that would be enough to save the tree? What do you think?" he looked so hopeful.

"I don't know. It would need to be official somewhere for the tree to be declared a historical landmark. I don't know if the women's journey had that much clout. Or Robert Frost, for that matter."

"I don't know either. Oh, I was able to make a few calls before I had to sleep off that pain medicine. I found out that at least one of our Linden Falls locals has an ancestor who fought at Gettysburg and that when he returned after his tour was up, he proposed to his sweetheart at the base of the Wishing tree. She had hung a wish for his safe return every single day that he was gone."

"That's so sweet," Coco said. "But it's not really history. Technically, I mean."

He looked glum.

"Don't worry. We've still got time to find out more. Let's get to work," Coco said.

"Before we do, can I ask a favor?"

"Sure."

"Can you help me take a shower?"

Coco didn't know what came over her but before she could stop them, her cheeks burned hot. It wasn't like he was asking her on a date for Pete's sake! It was just a shower.

Calvin noticed. He held his hands up. "Whoa. I just meant I need you to help wrap my leg. I swear, you won't have to see me in my birthday suit."

She played it off like he was being silly and laughed.

But for a minute, she'd been worried. She was doing Calvin a professional favor—well, many of them, until he got better.

When she left Linden Falls, she would be telling both him and Orson goodbye, and she hoped he didn't think it was going to pan out any differently.

CHAPTER 11

Janie was pouring over the inn's online ledger when Max came through the door of her shop. She looked up briefly, then back at the spreadsheet, searching for any way she could manipulate the numbers to find an extra several thousand dollars to save their tree.

"We're back. Just in case you were wondering. And no broken legs, Ma." He stopped at the display of candles and picked one up. He took the lid off and smelled the candle, then turned to her.

"Where are the girls?"

"Breeze said she wanted to take a hot bath, and Carly had a trillion text messages to answer since she didn't have her phone on the slopes. Seemed very important."

Janie snorted. "Right. They always are."

He put down the candle, then picked another and

turned to her. "How does someone know what candle to pick?"

Robotically, she answered him. "White candles can be for anything, but they are best for manifesting and attracting. Black is for repelling and banishing. Red for passion, green for money, blue for peace, etc."

She had a green one burning now. It couldn't hurt and she would love it if she could contribute to saving the tree.

He raised his eyebrows. "That's pretty detailed but what are people trying to manifest or repel? It sounds very mysterious."

She shrugged. Max would never understand, and she wasn't going to waste her breath trying to convince a doubter.

He approached the counter and leaned on it, his chin in his hands as he looked thoughtful. She could smell his cologne. What man wore cologne to go skiing? Max—that's who.

"I'm trying to grasp what this is all about, Janie. I want to know what it is you left your life for—our life for. Are telling me you're a witch? Is that it?" he asked.

Janie laughed. He looked so worried that it really tickled her funny bone and she wished so badly that she had a crystal ball and cauldron she could pull out.

Maybe even a pointed hat.

"Don't you think you've lived with me long enough to know if I'm a witch or not, Max? But to answer your question, we all have an innate sense of spirituality and can choose how to use it. For me, I've made a conscious decision to begin a path of being harmonious with my spirit, and with mother nature."

"Can you tell me that again, but this time in English?"

"Max, seriously? I don't have time for this."

"Just try once more," he said. "How does that compute to you walking away from a successful career and marriage?"

Janie closed her laptop. She wasn't going to get any numbers crunched with him in her store. "I'm definitely not a witch. But I want to do work that is of value."

He looked surprised. "You make amazing money at what you do!"

"I'm not talking about value in my bank account. I mean of value to the world. I want to contribute something to society that has a deeper meaning than the latest throw pillow design or a new line of wallpaper. I don't expect you to understand it because to be honest, I don't fully get it myself yet. I'm still working on who I want to be, but I do know that I don't want to be who I was."

He looked hurt. "And you can't work on yourself at home?"

"Max, look. I don't want to hurt you, and honestly, I don't understand why you're asking me this now. You agreed to a separation, and you said if I wanted it, a divorce. You are the one who was never home and who lived and breathed his work. I tried to tell you years ago how I felt about finding my birth father and even then, you told me not to dig around or I could end up finding something I wasn't prepared for. You were not supportive. I didn't listen and I'm glad I didn't. Because I found this place. And Neva. And hopefully—a part of me that has wanted to come alive and never had the chance to."

He fiddled with the colorful wrappers on the incense sticks she had in a jar next to the register. Janie could tell he had more to say but didn't know how to say it.

Max looked up. "And the girls. You're willing to make them grow up with a broken family?"

Oh, that was low.

"Come on, Max. Stop trying to guilt me. We won't be a broken family unless you make it that way. People co-parent successfully all the time. Carly will barely be around after next year, and Breeze will adjust once we show her it can be done and that we are partners in parenting. When they are older and married, we will still all gather for holidays. You with your significant other, and if I have one, me with mine. Furthermore, don't you dare try to use the girls to guilt me, especially when you've barely had five minutes of family time over a stretch of two years. Admit it, we grew apart."

"You have a new significant other?" he looked crestfallen.

Janie leaned her head back and stared at the ceiling, counting to five before she answered. "No, I don't. And I don't plan to. I'm talking about way in the future, and I know for sure you won't stay single."

"Why would you say that?"

"Because for one, you need someone to organize your personal life. Social things. Medical appointments. I bet you don't even know who our health insurance is with. And I know you have no idea how to file a claim. You are much too buried in your job to handle anything else. Instead, it was all on me."

"All of what?" he crossed his arms.

"All of anything and everything it takes to run a household for four. Do you want specifics? How much time do you have?"

He heard the irritation and backed off. Literally and figuratively.

"This shop looks great, Janie. I'm really impressed." He looked around.

"Thank you." She said, her voice cool. Flattery would get him nowhere. Especially when he'd ignited her temper.

He walked all the way to the far wall and saw the bucket she had out.

"What's going on back here?" he asked.

"Nothing. Isn't it time for you to go? I've got work to do." Max would be the one to spot the one imperfection in her shop. Okay, maybe not the only one but at least the one that had the most potential to be a big problem.

"I see water in it. The roof is leaking?"

"A teeny tiny leak. Nothing to worry over. I'm going to get Carly's friend Jonathon to fix it when he has time."

He found the stairs to the loft and went up to try to get closer.

"A tiny leak can become a huge one in the right storm conditions. Are you sure that a friend of Carly's has the experience to do it right? Wait—I see where it's coming from," he called out.

The front door opened, and two ladies entered the store. They wore visors and fanny packs, and one carried a bag with the Townsquare Books logo. "Hi. Are you open?"

"I sure am," Janie said, smiling at them both. When they turned to browse the candle table, she beckoned at Max to go.

He came down the stairs and approached her counter again.

"Okay, I'm leaving. But before I go let me tell you this," he said. "You should write a letter of objection to the city council and get Neva to sign it, as I'm sure she's one of the oldest living residents of Linden Falls. At the same time, we start a petition to change policies for your town trees, whether on private property or public. We rally the townspeople to get involved in whatever way they can."

"You let me worry about my town," Janie said, even though she knew she was being unpleasant, and Max truly did know things about things like this.

He smiled gently at her, and she hated the instant forgiveness he gave. It made her feel like a real jerk.

"Fine. See you at dinner?"

She didn't reply. It wouldn't do to encourage him

when they both knew it was too late for their relationship. They wanted different lives, and Janie sure didn't want to go back to Max's way of living. Or of feeling invisible.

"Okay, I'll take that as a yes," he said, then smiled at her and walked out the door.

CHAPTER 12

Over the next few weeks Janie found her life taking on a new rhythm. Once the breakfast chores were over and she'd finished checking in or out guests, she spent the rest of the morning working in her shop before closing it at two o'clock to help get ready for the inn's afternoon tea crowd.

Neva usually popped in after visiting the tree to let her know if any more donations had come in. Since the meeting she'd found personal checks hanging from a branch here or there, and people were doing what they could, but it wasn't enough, and the clock was counting down fast.

Janie didn't want to give up, but it wasn't looking good.

She took another comforting sip of the hot, steaming Maple Latte that she'd made. Carly had created the concoction and it was a hit for some of those who attended their tea parties but weren't fond of tea. Janie found it intoxicatingly delicious—the straight shot of pure Vermont maple syrup giving it an authentically sweet taste. She was going to have to watch herself with them, though, or she was going to need to go up a size in pants.

Max and the girls had left earlier for Doc's Fountain for ice cream, leaving her twiddling her thumbs until she'd decided to use her time wisely. Max had taken on looking over their schoolwork to keep them on track, giving Janie even more free time. He still hadn't gone home, and he explained it by saying that the company was re-structuring and hadn't taken on any new event contracts. He said he'd asked for an extended vacation and because of years of service, they'd granted it.

Janie had to admit, he'd made himself very useful since he'd been in Linden Falls. In addition to helping with the girls, he hadn't given up on doing what he could to save the Wishing tree. He'd drafted the letter of objection to its demise and though the city council had immediately replied and said it was out of their hands, at least they'd tried.

As Max had suggested, they'd also started a petition that was going around town now. Most of the shopkeepers were pushing it to their customers, and the girls were taking it door-to-door and catching the locals who didn't venture out much. So far, they had more than three hundred signatures but according to Max, it might not be enough.

As for funds to pay for the intricate root removal, they were nowhere near close to having enough. So many of the locals had stepped up to help raise what they could; Steve and Pam from the gym were doing special fitness classes and Verity was giving cooking lessons. The Winey Widows had held multiple bake sales and some of the residents of the Aspen Senior center had donated art they'd done to be auctioned off at the next craft fair.

It just wasn't enough. Not yet.

But she wasn't giving up. Still, there were other things to keep up with. Life didn't just stop with the crisis of the Wishing tree, though sometimes she felt like it should.

She opened another box from her small shipment that had arrived the day before. Receiving new merchandise never ceased to cheer her up. The shop was feeling more and more like her baby—a project that was something just for her.

Today it was wooden manifestation magnets. She loved that each one was handmade and purchased from a mom across the country who worked from home so that she could be there full-time for her son who has autism. Janie loved supporting her small business because not only did it help the woman financially, but it also showed her that her artistic efforts were appreciated. That she was more than just a harried mom, she was a creator.

The magnets came engraved with two sayings. One said *"it's already yours. Signed, the Universe."* And the other said *"Make it Happen. Signed, the Universe."*

She carefully priced and then placed each one on

the metal backboard she'd hung just the evening before when she'd worked late rearranging the displays.

A sudden banging startled her, and Janie jumped.

There was a pause and then it began again, a rhythm of three strikes, then pause. A few seconds wait and then again. Three strikes.

What in the world?

She went outside and looked around but didn't see anything.

When it started again, she realized it was coming from above and she looked up to see Max kneeling on the roof of the shop.

"What are you doing up there?" she called out.

He paused, hammer in the air. "Good morning, Sunshine. As you can see, I'm fixing your roof. There was a small hole under a rotted shingle, so I patched it. Now I'm replacing some of the other older shingles, so you don't have deal with any more leaks for a long time. I need to look at the roof on the main house too."

Janie put her hands on her hips. What was she going to say? If she thanked him, he'd think he won.

She opted to divert the conversation. "I thought you and the girls were getting ice cream?"

He rubbed his belly and smiled. "Already did. They make the best root beer float I've ever had, and the server was so hospitable. She made it such an enjoyable experience."

Janie knew who he was talking about. It was a new woman in town, probably about her own age. She also knew Max had never even had a root beer float. As a matter of fact, he was always gone or too busy to accompany her and the girls on ice cream runs.

Was he trying to make her jealous? She had to admit though, he looked good up there dressed in his new old-looking jeans and flannel checkered shirt. Not only was he dressing different these days, but he'd traded his sleek black car for a four-wheel drive Jeep Cherokee.

But none of that was any of her business anymore. He didn't have to discuss financial decisions with his soon-to-be ex.

"Thank you for patching the leak, Max. But I could've hired someone to do that. You don't need to be climbing around and chance getting hurt. You have to get back to the city and to work."

He cupped a hand to his ear. "Can't hear you. I'll talk to you when I come down!"

She knew he'd heard her, but she turned around and went back into the store.

Inside, she returned to the box of magnets and finished hanging them. She felt conflicted about Max. Of course, she was thankful that he was helping. On the other hand, he was being the kind of partner she'd wanted for so long, and then given up on. It was too late and now she had her own thing going. She was enjoying her independence. And she was enjoying feeling close to her roots in Linden Falls. She looked forward to exploring the state more. There was so much to do. She'd promised the girls they'd visit the Morgan horse farm soon and attend the upcoming hot air balloon festival.

Then Carly wanted to go to Stowe and see the haunted Emily's Bridge, where allegedly the ghost of a young woman who hanged herself from the bridge comes back to haunt pedestrians who cross. Apparently, some of her friends from home had told her about it and now Carly wanted the prestige of claiming she'd seen it.

Janie couldn't let her go alone.

And anyway, she wanted to do a girl's road trip before Carly took off across the world. Neva had told her that route 100 wound through the whole state of Vermont and was the best way to see all the fall foliage, with cool places to stop along the way.

First, though, she had to get her shop going well and find someone to fill in while they were away, both in the shop and at the inn. She couldn't leave Neva to handle all of it. It was funny, she thought her life in Linden Falls was so much simpler than she had in the city, but it did come with its own set of responsibilities.

The door swung open, and Carly came rushing in, Breeze in hot pursuit behind her.

"Mom, there are work trucks at the square and one has a cherry-picker. I think they are going to try to take the tree down early," she said.

"No, they can't do that! We have one more week." They didn't have nearly enough signatures on the petition yet to even get the city council to blink an eye. Not only that, but despite everyone pitching in to do what they could to raise funds, they still didn't have enough for the specialized procedure to repair the pipes that the roots of the tree had damaged.

"I don't know but Neva is already there trying to stop them. She told me to come back and get you and Dad. He's climbing down now."

Janie felt her heart in her throat, but she hurried to the door, flipped the sign to *Closed* and followed the girls outside.

Max was already on the ground, talking to Coco.

"That's a great idea," she was saying.

"What's a great idea?" Janie cut in. "We have to hurry. I don't want Neva to get too upset there alone."

"Coco works in television and has connections back home. She's going to try to get a news team out there and get some outside influence," Max said. He turned back to Coco. "Pitch it as a human-interest story, or whatever you have to do to get them to send a camera crew."

He was in professional mode. Janie could see it all over his face and this time, she was glad he was there.

"Okay, let me go make some calls. I'll meet you there," Coco said, then hurried into the house.

CHAPTER 13

Coco was glad that Linden Falls had small town habits because when she tried to open the door on Constable Pike's car, it was unlocked. The locals were already gathering around the tree, and Neva was in the middle of the fray, and though Coco couldn't hear what was being said, it appeared that the slight woman was giving the four workman a piece of her mind.

Constable Pike stood with them, looking very nervous.

The obvious leader of the work crew had taken his safety helmet off and was holding it against his middle, nodding as Neva spoke. The other three stood a few feet behind, looking nervously at the crowd.

Coco grabbed what she was looking for from a box in the constable's floorboard and made her way to the tree. As she went, she quickly sent Calvin a text to let him know what was happening.

"You have to give us more time," Neva was saying to the foreman.

"Respectfully, ma'am, we don't. We have our orders," he replied. "Now if you'll step back out of the way, we also have a tight schedule. The plumbing team are coming next and if we get behind, they'll get behind, and everyone will be working late and miss dinner with their families. You don't want that, do you?"

"Ms. Cabot, I'm so sorry but he's right. They have a legal right to do what has been ordered by the property owner. We can't stop them."

Coco bypassed all of them and took the roll of orange tape and tied the end to a low-hanging branch. Then with it in hand, she began walking around the tree in a wide circle, weaving the tape over and under other branches to keep it at waist level.

A hush fell over the growing crowd, Neva, and the workmen as they watched her.

When she got to where she'd started, she stepped behind the tape and then finished the circle, tearing off the end before tying it off.

Now she leaned against the tree, within the circle of orange tape.

"Ma'am, you need to move," the foreman said, a dark look coming across his face.

"No, I don't. I'm not going anywhere and if you're going to cut down this tree, you'll take me with it."

Constable Pike straightened to his full height. "Now listen here. I'm not familiar with who you are and why you feel you need to be involved in this situation, but you can't do that. Playing the role of a tree-hugger isn't going to do any good. And is that my tape?"

Coco didn't even know why she felt she needed to be so involved, but she did. And she wasn't admitting to anything.

Suddenly she saw Max and Janie, and their girls arrive. She beckoned to Carly.

When they got to the tree, she handed Carly her phone.

"You are the best with this kind of stuff, and social media, so I need you to start filming when I say go, okay? I called my friend, Travis, but it will take him at least another hour to get here so we're going to have to do it without him."

Carly nodded. "What do I say?"

"You don't say anything. I'll do the talking. But don't start until I give you the signal. First I want to make sure there are as many locals here as possible."

Max looked grim and Janie looked ashen. Breeze ran to Neva and wrapped her arms around her, burying her face against her chest.

She was crying and that tore Coco's heart out.

The constable started lecturing Coco, but Neva gave her a grateful smile.

"Do what you can dear, but I don't want you to get hurt," she said.

Coco didn't listen to what was being said as she was trying to get straight in her head what she was going to say. Her thoughts were a circle of chaos, and she forgot all the research she'd dug up. Suddenly the names and historical tidbits flew out of her head and now she was going to look ridiculous for simply tying herself to a tree without a backup plan.

She needed to get herself together. She'd had no plans of trying to do a special piece and with her luck, it would go nowhere, but she didn't have time for anything more professional, so she was going to have to do her best.

If she could just figure out what that best was.

As more townspeople gathered around, the foreman and the constable started arguing. Susan Crawford and her husband showed up and joined the work crew and took up verbal sparring with a few more people that Coco didn't know.

Soon the buzz of voices got louder.

When Coco saw a break in the crowd of people and watched them step aside to let someone through, her anxiety began to melt off.

Calvin had found a way there and was struggling but working his way down to the tree on the crutches and he'd locked eyes with her.

Finally, he was close enough to lean in and talk to her.

"Great idea, Coco. Right now, you're our only chance."

That didn't help.

"But I don't know what to say," she began. "You know this town. And this tree. I think you should do the talking and Carly will get it recorded, then I can see if I can get a local station to pick it up. This could be big for you if it does get picked up. You could get a promotion, or another job somewhere else."

She also thought about what her boss, Frank, had said about her. How she didn't depict what a newswoman should look like.

Calvin shook his head. "I'm not a talker. I can't do it. I didn't tell you this, but the reason I never tried to go further in this career is because every time I tried to be in front of the camera, my childhood stutter came back. It wasn't worth it to me to try to overcome it. I'm happy being a reporter."

She felt terrible for him. For his secret. "But Calvin, there are specialists for that now. They can help."

"I don't want more than what I have here, Coco. I'm satisfied with my life. With the balance of it. I know that's hard for someone like you to understand, but I'm more than what I do for a living. I like being with friends. Hanging out with my grandfather. Taking long walks with Orson. I want to enjoy life—not race around spending every minute working. But this isn't about me. It's about saving the tree. And I need your help. Will you do it?"

She looked around at all of them.

Neva. Janie and Max. The girls.

They all waited for her to say something.

To do something.

She dug in her pocket and found the gemstone that Janie had sold her. She clutched it in her hand then nodded. "Okay. Let's do it."

Max shushed the crowd, and Coco took a deep breath and began talking.

"The Linden Falls Wishing tree goes back to the days when the main street was laid with cobblestones and traveled by horse and buggy, the townspeople visited wooden storefronts to fill their pantries, and the tree's limbs and leaves were whipped about in slight breezes and hefty hurricanes. It has withstood the hardest of times and remained as rooted to the Linden Falls ground as many of your families have. And now a fancy business owner wants to just chop it down and let it die."

Calvin gave her an encouraging nod and Coco paused to gather more thoughts.

"All over the state, small towns are disappearing into the shadows of sprawling cities, modern technology and commercialism. While many people think that development is for the best of civilization, what they neglect to remember is that civilization is not about business and money. Civilization comes down to how we treat each other. To being good neighbors and having tolerance for one another. From honoring memories and traditions and taking forth the lessons we've learned. This tree has been a part of all of that and deserves to remain so."

She told them about the women end-to-enders hikers. She talked about how the tree was a part of marking their achievement and the inspiration they gave to other women who wanted to do more than wear an apron and make biscuits. Women who would later be noted for their brilliance and contribution to culture.

"Trees and humans have a close relationship because we keep each other alive. We keep them healthy so they can give us materials to live with and they filter the air to help our breathing. Taking a healthy tree away for the sake of money is just sacrilege."

Then she reminded them of the great flood of 1927 and how many of them were here today because of the sheer tenacity their ancestors had to survive, some of whom climbed up and sought safety and clutched the very branches of their Wishing tree until their fingers were bloody and the storm was over. Even when the bridges and roads were washed away, and eighty-four other lives were lost, the tree stood up against the whipping winds to protect the people depending on it.

She mentioned sweethearts made and proposals accepted under the tree, marriages and babies and multiple generations that wishes tied to the branches had brought about. Of wives and mothers of men sent to battle, who wrote them long letters as they lay beneath the tree, hanging wishes of safety and planning their reunions.

She saw a trio of older ladies look thrilled when she recanted how she'd read about Robert Frost, and his stay and then the poem he wrote about wishes, that could indeed be referring to their special tree.

As Coco spoke, remembering details she'd unearthed at the library, she felt herself standing taller, feeling stronger with every word until she busted out of the police tape and lifted her fist into the air.

"They cannot have this tree!" she exclaimed.

The crowd roared with agreement and Carly turned, capturing faces filled with pride and tears, and courage before she brought it back to Coco.

"Linden Falls is special," she continued.

Susan Crawford stepped forward. "Yes, it is. It's not the tree that makes us. It's the town. It will continue to be special even with the tree gone."

Paige Duncan shushed her, then waved at Coco to keep going.

Coco did. "And this tree has been a huge part in making it that way. It is the roots of the small town and the tree that has passed along all of its good traits from generation to generation, encouraging the people not to be swept up in the bad news and crimes of the bigger cities," Coco said. "Choosing instead to embrace the magic of the tree that protects it's people; bringing them hope, forgiveness, and love."

A murmur swept through the crowd.

Suddenly Coco felt a flutter around her head and reached up to protect herself. It was that blasted bird again, this time interrupting what would've been a magical moment caught on video.

"Go away," she exclaimed. But the bird flew around her again, then landed on the trunk of the tree and started pecking away at it. It was pretty. Startling with its black and white coat, and bright red crest with a bill that looked like a small trumpet.

But it was not a good time. Coco struggled to remember what she'd been saying. She looked to Calvin, and he nodded encouragingly.

Carly looked uncertain about what to do but before Coco could get her on track, a woman in the crowd stepped forward and came closer, peering up at the tree.

"I can't even believe it," she said, then turned to the man with her. "Walt, is that what I think it is?"

He scrutinized the bird behind Coco, then busted out in a smile that spread across his face. He grabbed his wife and swung her around, laughing. "It sure is, Lee."

Carly swung to them to capture what he said.

He pointed at the tree, urging Carly to see it. "Folks, that's the first Ivory-billed Woodpecker to be spotted since 1944. It's North America's largest woodpecker and has been officially declared extinct, but I'd bet my entire bird-watching career that what I'm seeing is indeed true. The Good Lord Bird is not dead!"

Neva smiled at Coco. "You know what this means, don't you?"

"What?" Coco said.

"Our Wishing tree has given us a miracle."

CHAPTER 14

A week after the near demise of their Wishing tree, Janie lifted her glass of wine and gave a toast to the two heroes at the table. It was a celebratory dinner and this time, they were at the French restaurant in town and Carly was being served instead of cooking in the kitchen. Her video skills had proven effective, or perhaps it was the inspiring speech that Coco had given, but it had gone viral and not only was the tree saved, but the footage of the special bird had brought in thousands of birdwatchers from around the world.

Officials had stepped in and put a moratorium on anything that had to do with taking the tree down until the fate of the bird could be decided. That gave them more time to figure out a long-term plan.

"Thank you," Coco said, blushing brightly. She and Calvin sat at the end of the table and Janie noticed they'd been deep in conversation, looking at a tarot card since she'd sat down. "But I have one request."

They waited.

"My name is Courtney and I'd love to use it from now on, if you don't mind dropping the Coco."

Janie wasn't surprised. She'd never thought the name Coco had fit her anyway.

The viral video, which was now her second viral video, after the one of her embarrassing accident at the gym, had also brought Coco's boss to town. She'd talked to him, albeit briefly, then come back into the house with a confident look of triumph.

"First he tried to butter me up by telling me how much slimmer I look," Coco told them.

"You do look like you've lost a bit, dear," Neva said.

Coco looked down at herself. "Hmm.. maybe. I've been so busy running back and forth to the library for research, walking Orson, and helping Calvin at home that I've not stepped on the scale to check! But anyway, he offered me the news anchorwoman position and I turned it down. I'm staying in Linden Falls and I'm going to start a blog. Be an influencer, if I can. Well, that and help Calvin with the paper."

"Oh, I think you are well on your way to being an influencer," Janie said.

"She is. She's got almost as many followers as Anderson Cooper," Carly said.

"Who is Anderson Cooper?" Max asked, causing Carly to roll her eyes.

"Courtney, you don't need to worry about stepping

on any scales," Calvin said. "You looked perfect from the first moment I opened my eyes and saw you stooped over me in the street. It was worth breaking my leg, I promise you that."

They all oohed at his sweet talk and Calvin blushed.

Janie didn't know about the weight, but she didn't think Coco—oops. Calling her Courtney was going to take a while to get used to—realized how much she glowed compared to when she'd first arrived.

Courtney waved her hand. "Let's stop talking about me, please, and get back to the tree."

Max tilted his glass to Coco, then Carly. "You deserve the acknowledgement. Both of you. If you hadn't decided to film your speech, no one would've believed what happened."

"And thanks to Walt for recognizing the bird," Neva said.

"Hear, hear," Henry said, raising his glass again.

A week had passed since the day the Wishing tree was saved, but it had been such a whirlwind of activity that it felt like just moments ago.

They wouldn't have gotten a table since every establishment was overwhelmed with tourists now, but Janie had mentioned that the now infamous Coco Baines would be with them and that had opened a reservation immediately. The whole town was thankful to her for her part in saving the Wishing tree and since they'd seen her face splashed all over every news channel, felt like they had a celebrity among them.

Calvin adjusted his sweater vest and lifted his glass

for a second toast. "To the Ivory-billed Woodpecker. For coming back from the dead long enough to save our tree."

Neva chuckled. "I just can't believe it. And I think I may not have if the Cornell Laboratory of Ornithology had not confirmed it."

"Don't forget about the Nature Conservancy, too," Leona said. "It's true. And yes, it is indeed a miracle that the Ivory-Billed Woodpecker has been taken off the extinct list."

"Downgraded back to endangered," Walt said.

"How did it become endangered in the first place?" Breeze asked.

Walt cleared his throat before beginning. "Way back in the 1800's those birds became scarce when the forests and pine woods they nest in were cleared for lumber or for farming. Then hunters took after them, claiming it to be holy grail of birds to have as a stuffed trophy. Between the loggers and the hunters, they put them on the endangered list."

Leona nodded. "There were still some in northeast Louisiana on a tract of woods owned by the Singer sewing company, and research was done on them there, but eventually Singer took that tract down too. They needed the wood to make frames for sewing machines in the early 40's."

"That's really sad," Janie said. "And one more example of how trees were annihilated for the sake of lining someone's pocket and to the detriment of life around it."

"What will happen to the bird now?" Carly asked.

"They are coming up with a plan," Walt said. "I'm sure the bird will continue to be under strict surveillance so they can see if it has more of its kind somewhere."

"They might even capture it and take it to a safe refuge," Leona said. "We just don't know at this point, and I guess we shouldn't speculate."

"If the bird leaves, will they try to take the tree down again?" Carly asked.

"There is a slim chance that the tree and area around it will be designated as a Critical Habitat since the bird was found there. That would enable it to be safe to allow for the possibility of future sightings of the woodpecker there," Walt said.

"But like he said, it's a slim chance," his wife added.

"I don't think we are going to have to worry about that," Max said.

All eyes turned to him.

"Why not?" Janie asked.

"Because I bought the King property from the new owners, and I won't be a jerk about getting the plumbing fixed as quickly as they wanted it done."

The sudden silence was deafening.

"What do you mean, you bought it?" Janie finally said.

"Just what I said. I bought it. The people that were going to put in the sports bar were eager to take my offer and stop trying to fight against what they felt was a losing battle. They said even if they won and the tree came down, their business would probably suffer because it wouldn't have the townspeople's support."

"How did you find out who it was?" Neva asked.

"I didn't know until the offer was accepted. I sent word through the mayor."

"Well, I wonder what Susan Wilbanks will set her sights on next," Neva mumbled.

"You knew, too?" Janie exclaimed.

Neva frowned. "Phsht. Of course, I knew. Her absence from everything was a red flag considering she's usually right in the middle of anything and everything. She's not a very smart one."

They laughed. Janie knew that for Neva to talk disparagingly about anyone was unusual and her obvious dislike for Susan Crawford seemed to be shared around the table.

"I have an idea for what we are going to do with the King building now," Max said. "After we finally get the plumbing repaired."

We.

Janie didn't know who he thought *we* was, but she already had a business and a half. And he wasn't going to be able to go back and forth from the city. She was interested to know what his plan was.

"King Artisan Market." He looked smug with himself.

"We already have a farmer's market where a lot of people sell their wares," Janie said.

"This is going to be more than that. Fancier. I plan to renovate the inside with a very rustic and Vermont-like décor. Something that is cozy and inviting, that will make people want to come to town just to spend the afternoon there. There will even be a roaring fire in the cold months, once we build the fireplace."

"What will be sold inside?" Leona asked.

"Part of the building will have booths for artists to display their work. Anything from paintings to pottery to quilts. Anything that takes creative talent. The other part of the building will be rented out for various fairs and visiting craft shows. Possibly even author events, seeing how Vermont is known as a writer's retreat."

"I think it's a splendid idea, Max," Neva said, clapping her hands together excitedly.

"I second that," Henry added, smiling down at Neva.

"Third," both Carly and Breeze said at the same time.

"Jinx." They both spoke again.

Janie knew they had savings, but she didn't know what it had cost to buy the property. She couldn't very well be angry at Max for buying it without telling her. He was doing it for the town, and what he did with his part of their money shouldn't matter to her anymore.

"But what about the roots of the tree? Do we still need to raise money for the special procedure?" Courtney asked.

"I think if we put out a donation box, the birdwatchers will fill it up fast!" Calvin said. "We should've already thought of that."

"That will help, and have you all heard about the book?" Neva asked. "Paige and her fiancé, Reed, just signed a deal with one of the top five publishers of children's books. Reed has written a story about the miracle of the Wishing tree, and Paige is illustrating it. It will appeal to bird lovers as well as children who will love reading about wishes and the magic of the tree. They are donating all the proceeds to the tree."

"Wow—that's so great," Janie said. "And I love that they get to do it together."

Max said. "Well, on that note, I need an interior designer to help my vision come together for the Artisan Market. We could do it together, Janie. Really make it special."

Janie was saved from answering him when he pulled out a piece of thick paper and handed it to Neva.

"One more thing," Max said.

"What is this?" Neva asked.

"A deed and it's my last surprise tonight. During some of our talks, you expressed concern about the next time something gets stirred up about the tree, and if you aren't here and someone in power decides to do the unthinkable without even talking to the next generation of Linden Falls."

She nodded sadly. "It's true. Right now, we have some good people in official positions, but what if someone like the Susan Wilbanks takes over as mayor? Someone who doesn't understand how special the tree is. I have to admit, it's worries like those that keep me up at night."

"Then you're going to like what I found out," Max said. "While I was doing research on how to repair the pipes without cutting the roots, I read about a tree in Athens, Georgia. It owns itself after Colonel William Henry Jackson deeded the land around it back to it in the 1800s. He had such fond memories of the tree during his childhood that he wanted to make sure no one would ever try to hurt it. I've checked into it and the city council has approved my suggestion to deed the land surrounding the tree, to the tree. It will no longer be owned by the city, and no one will ever be able to touch it, no matter who comes into power in Linden Falls."

Janie could see Neva trying not to cry. Henry reached over and put his arm around her shoulders and pulled her close. Everyone around the table looked overcome with emotion.

"Daddy, that's so nice. And you kept it a secret!" Carly said, laughing.

"It is nice, but I don't understand why you've done all this? You don't know Linden Falls that well, and you don't have any roots here," Courtney said.

Max looked over the table, locking eyes with Janie.

"You are wrong. I do have ties to Linden Falls because my wife does. And my wife is the strongest, most stubborn, kindest, generous and compassionate person I know. I was a fool to take her for granted and to ever let her leave. And I will spend the rest of my life doing my best to make it up to her and show her how much I appreciate her. Everything I did here is for her —a gesture to show my devotion to Janie's emotional wellbeing."

"Max..." Janie didn't want him to do this. Not here, especially.

He held a hand up. "No, let me finish. I want to say it all right here and right now. In front of God, our children, everyone at this table, and the whole blasted town if need be. I want *everyone* to know I've been a fool and I'm ready to make amends."

"I'm ready to go," Janie said, looking for their server for the check.

"Let him talk, Mama," Carly whispered across the table.

"Yeah," chimed in Breeze.

Janie's cheeks burned hot when Max pushed his chair back, got up and came around the table. He knelt in front of her, then took her hand.

"Janie Marie Stallard, my love. My soul mate and my reason for living. I was stupid. And so blind. But living in our house without you, without the girls, it showed me what is important in life. It's not money or prestige, or the next biggest event. It's us. As a family. Not in a house, or two houses apart. But together, in one home."

Janie didn't dare look at her girls.

Max continued. "I resigned from my job, Janie."

Her eyes widened. He loved his job.

"But why?" she asked.

"That job means nothing to me if I don't have you. I've already started the process of forming my own business for event organizing. But smaller ones I can do here and the surrounding area. Never again any of the big ones that will take me away from you or the girls through distance or by sacrificing our family time. I want to be with you, wherever you are. And I'm excited about becoming a real resident of Linden Falls, and a business owner here. I love this place and I want to know my neighbors. Lend a helping hand. Make friends. Borrow a cup of sugar."

"Daddy, you don't eat sugar," Breeze said.

He laughed. "You're right, kiddo. But I'll explain later. Give me a second to convince your mom to give me one more chance."

Janie didn't speak. Everyone was waiting for her to say something, and the pressure was crushing. Max could see it, too.

"Do you want to think about it some more? I'm sorry that I put you on the spot. I just couldn't wait another minute to say what I needed to say. It's been burning a hole in my chest."

He looked so earnest. She remembered the first time she'd ever seen him. She was on the interstate, and he was driving a convertible. He passed her, then moved over and slowed down so much she had to pass him.

When he hollered through the window and asked for her number, he'd had the same earnest look and she'd thrown caution to the wind and yelled it out to him. Then she hit the gas and could see him in the mirror, repeating the number over and over to himself. She figured he'd forget it before he could find something to write it down with. But he didn't.

He'd called and asked her out. Insisted even, and from their first date, she'd known he was the one. It was a whirlwind engagement and quick wedding. Then the girls came, and things got tough as they tried to build their life. Time together got harder to find between diaper changes, jobs, homework, and the million other things that came into play with a growing family and two careers.

Eventually, when things could've slowed down and instead, he worked harder and longer, she thought Max had outgrown her. That he wanted to be with more successful people, wining and dining, strutting his success. Her own success had fueled her for a while. Or at least until she realized that her soul was hungry for more. More than money or building a brand. Things that Max wasn't interested in.

"Before you answer, I have something else to say," Max said. "Garnet is for healing, Moonstone is for intuition, Citrine is for clarity and Bloodstone can help lessen feelings of anger, hostility and impatience."

Janie couldn't help but laugh. Max was blowing her mind!

"But how—when?"

"I've been studying," he said. "I know I was guiding us wrong by chasing material wealth without working to make our lives balanced in other ways. And I'm open to learning more from you, or by myself, or from whomever wants to teach me. As long as that means I can keep you. And I promise to never ask if you are a witch again."

That brought out nervous laughter, as the others weren't in on the joke.

"The ring, Daddy," Carly whispered.

"Oh, I almost forgot!" he winked at her and Breeze, then dug in his pocket and brought out a gorgeous emerald ring. "The emerald is for rebirth and compassion. I think it can represent this new path in our relationship. If you'll accept it."

Janie looked to Neva.

Neva shook her head. "I can't tell you on this one, dear girl. You have to follow your heart."

Janie turned to Courtney, then blinked to clear her eyes. Yes, she was seeing it right. Calvin had scooted his chair as close to hers as possible and was holding her hand as they watched and listened. They were definitely a couple now.

Neva was right once again. She'd predicted they'd be lovebirds the very morning that she'd sent Courtney to Calvin's house with Orson.

Breeze and Carly were unnaturally quiet, waiting for Janie to speak.

It would be easy for her to say yes for them. Because they wanted their mom and dad together. They wanted it so badly you could see the hope shining in their eyes. And Janie had always tried to give them everything their hearts desired.

But this time, she had to live for herself. The girls would be gone one day and with them, Janie's youth. She didn't want to waste any more time with someone who would not be her forever.

Max kept her gaze without flinching. He'd said all the things she'd wanted to hear for so long but had always thought was just wishful thinking.

She thought of her new shop. And the inn.

All the people she loved in Linden Falls.

The Wishing tree.

No doubt it had brought Max back to her.

Her heart told her that she'd never get Max out of her system, no matter how hard she tried. She remembered him on the roof of her shop, so eager to help her and wearing a second-hand leather toolbelt he'd picked up. He'd looked deliciously manly. So much so that she'd had to turn away and pretend that he was just someone she knew, and not the one she lay awake thinking of half the night. Yes, he still had the ability to tease her senses.

All of them.

There really was no other decision to be had.

She held her hand out and Max slid the ring on her finger.

It was a perfect fit for her.

Just like Max.

OVERDUE WISHES SNEAK PEEK

Neva stepped out of the inn and onto the porch to give it a quick sweep. Breeze had watered her flowers and pinched off the old blooms, and the entrance was almost ready.

That would be one task knocked off the list, but Neva still had so much to do to prepare for the guests that would soon begin arriving for the All-Class Reunion to be held in Linden Falls the next day. You could feel the energy of the town as all around her, everyone hustled and bustled, preparing their shops and restaurants while work crews prepped to get tables, tents, and a stage set up for the big event.

There was anticipation in the air and though everyone was busy, the mood around them was joyful. It was always a fun time when the townspeople pulled together to welcome visitors, no matter what it was for.

Janie and the girls had come up with a grand idea and were busy redecorating the tearoom to emulate a vintage high school prom. Breeze had made a list of the hit songs from that era, and they'd even gone through Neva's old yearbooks and photocopied pictures, then plastered them into a photo booth that Max and Henry had built for the occasion.

Carly was working on a candy bar laden with old favorites famous during that time like Pixy Stix, Hot Tamales, and Atomic Fireballs. There would even be marshmallow Peeps and Black Taffy. Fizzies and Smarties candy necklaces.

Neva nearly giggled at the thought of many of her old friends wearing the sweets around their neck as though they were still chatty schoolgirls.

The inn would get a lot of foot traffic and her goal was to make guests feel like they were stepping back into time.

Neva hoped that Norma would be pleased with their efforts.

Speaking of her good friend, she spotted her across the square and waved.

Norma was setting up her reunion visitor's booth. She waved back and then turned her attention to her clipboard. They couldn't have picked a more detailed or organized person to take on coordinating the reunion. Norma wasn't only the best librarian Neva had ever known, but she had a talent for making sure a myriad of details was pulled together to make every project she took on look smooth and easy.

Neva was relieved to only handle what went on at the inn, and not look after everything else that went into making the reunion a smashing success.

A breeze gently danced up and around, and the sudden fluttering of wishes tied to the town tree caught Neva's attention.

Norma pulled her cardigan together as though suddenly chilled, then she trudged to her car and picked up one of the many plastic totes stacked in the back. She carried it over to her booth and set it down, then opened it and began cataloguing what it contained against a list on her clipboard.

Neva stopped sweeping and rested her chin on the top of her broomstick, watching her friend and recollecting that over the years, Norma led a somewhat discreet existence. It was almost as though she purposely tried not to draw attention to herself. Norma was kind and giving, and she always lent a helping hand, but she did it quietly and expected no fanfare for her contributions.

And come to think of it, Neva couldn't remember ever pulling a wish off the tree that was written by Norma.

The breeze rustled even higher, and the tree seemed to beckon, leaning toward Norma as though handing out an invitation, beseeching and promising that wishing wasn't something set aside only for others, but was offered to Norma as well.

Norma stopped what she was doing and stared at the tree, scrutinizing it for a moment.

Neva had a feeling that things were about to change for her good friend. And change could be good, no matter what your age. Especially when the Linden Falls Wishing Tree had a hand—or a limb—in making it happen.

She smiled, then went back to sweeping.

To discover what's in store for Norma, read OVERDUE WISHES, the next book in series by Tammy L. Grace.

★ Don't miss a Wishing Tree book! ★

Book 1: The Wishing Tree – prologue book
Book 2: I Wish.. by Amanda Prowse
Book 3: Wish You Were Here by Kay Bratt
Book 4: Wish Again by Tammy L. Grace
Book 5: Workout Wishes & Valentine Kisses by Barbara Hinske
Book 6: A Parade of Wishes by Camille Di Maio
Book 7: Careful What You Wish by Ashley Farley
Book 8: Gone Wishing by Jessie Newton
Book 9: Wishful Thinking by Kay Bratt
Book 10: Overdue Wishes by Tammy L. Grace
Book 11: A Whole Heap of Wishes by Amanda Prowse
Book 12: Wishes of Home by Barbara Hinske
Book 13: Wishful Witness by Tonya Kappes

We also invite you to join us in our My Book Friends group on Facebook. It's a great place to chat about all things bookish and learn more about our founding authors.

FROM THE AUTHOR

Thank you so much for reading WISHFUL THINKING, the ninth book in THE WISHING TREE SERIES. I've had so much fun revisiting Linden Falls and picking Janie's story back up while adding in Coco Baines. I also enjoyed sprinkling tidbits in about Neva, as I've come to know and love her as though she were a real person who I wish I could have over for a steaming cup of Janie's special tea.

As for this story, I wrote it at a time when like Janie, I've really started to question the meaning of life and my role in it. For the last decade and more, I've worked much harder than I ever thought possible, reaching milestones and knocking out career goals. This is the 26th book I've finished writing! I've put in way too many hours at the computer and caused irreparable damage to my body in my quest to write as many books as I possibly can. Part of it is my constant struggle to prove that I'm more than I started out as, or many expected me to be.

Now in my fifth decade, I find myself questioning what it is all for. When I'm dead and gone, it will be the quality of my work and not the quantity that is remembered. I need to remember that as I go forward and take as much time as I need to figure out what message I'm trying to leave the readers—and possibly my great-great-grandchildren and those further down the line who get curious about me—with. I also need to take more time for myself, and I've begun doing that, using my free time to read about spiritual things and explore theories. I've found that the more I discover, the more I thirst to know.

I can't say I'm into tarot cards and healing stones like Janie stocks in her shop, but they probably have a place in this world for to those who genuinely understand them and use them for good and not evil. However, they are not on my path of spiritual growth.

Oh, and while I wish—no pun intended—that the Ivory-Billed Woodpecker was indeed discovered and no longer extinct, I should alert you that is not true. Sadly, so far no one has found any evidence to the contrary, but I did think it would be a great miracle for the Wishing tree to pull off, for remember, that tree has magic and capabilities that we cannot understand.

I have always loved trees. Years ago, I published a duology that starts out with a child being abandoned underneath a Willow tree. I also have a very special Willow of my own that I can see right now outside my window. My father brought it here and helped us plant it in memory of our special little gentleman dog who died last year. His name was Grandpa Oliver, and he has quite a story and had garnered a huge online fan club because of his tenacity and resilience. We were blessed to have him as part of our family for a brief time, and I believe we were the first to ever show him love.

He has sent signs to me from the other side to let me know he's still around, and that he's happy. You can read about it in my memoir, ALL MY DOGS GO TO HEAVEN, where I also delve into my tumultuous life. If you've lost a pet that is like a child to you, or know someone who has, reviews say it's been bringing comfort to many in those shoes.

If you have enjoyed *WISHFUL THINKING*... I hope that you'll take the time to post a short review on Amazon, Goodreads, or BookBub. Your reviews help my work get seen easier and are priceless to me as an author.

I've also many more books for you to choose from if you'd like to read more of my work. A fan favorite is the *By the Sea* series, which starts with TRUE TO ME and was inspired by my youngest daughter who I helped move to Maui.

And if you like to sink into a longer series, my TALES OF THE SCAVENGER'S DAUGHTERS has garnered over a quarter of a million readers and is loved by many.

If you aren't a series kind of reader, then WISH ME

FROM THE AUTHOR

HOME is a standalone and would be good for you to start with, especially if you love dogs.

See more works by me at my website: https://kaybratt.com

ABOUT THE AUTHOR

Photo © 2013 Eclipse Photography

Kay Bratt learned to lean on writing while she navigated a tumultuous childhood and then a decade of domestic abuse in adulthood. After working her way through the hard years to come out a survivor and a pursuer of peace, she finally found the courage to use her experiences throughout her novels, most recently Wish Me Home and True to Me. She lives with the love of her life and a pack of rescue dogs on banks of Lake Hartwell in Georgia, USA. For more information, visit www.kaybratt.com.

Printed in Great Britain
by Amazon